Praise for Lexxie Couper's
Love's Rhythm

"Brimming with humor and emotion...you'd best get out the ice water and fan, readying yourself for some hot rock-star lovin'."

~ *USA Today*

"Wonderful, amazing, riveting are just some of the adjectives that I could use to describe this book. I fell in love with it from the first page and stayed glued to this story until it ended. I laughed and cried and worried and rejoiced while reading this superb story."

~ *Night Owl Reviews*

"A sigh-worthy tale with plenty of witty dialogue, appealing characters, and a reunion to end all reunions. This story is a memorable read from start to finish and any contemporary romance reader who hasn't given Lexxie Couper's stories a try should most definitely do so."

~ *Long and Short Reviews*

Look for these titles by
Lexxie Couper

Now Available:

Death, The Vamp and His
Brother
The Sun Sword
Triple Dare
Dare Me
Suspicious Ways
Muscle for Hire

Savage Australia
Savage Retribution
Savage Transformation

Bandicoot Cove
Exotic Indulgence
Tropical Sin
Love's Rhythm
Sunset Heat

Party Games
Suck and Blow
Twister

Principatus
Dark Embrace

Print Anthologies
Red-Hot Winter
Tropical Desires
Red Hot Weekend
Tropical Haze

Love's Rhythm

Lexxie Couper

SAMHAIN PUBLISHING

Samhain Publishing, Ltd.
11821 Mason Montgomery Road, 4B
Cincinnati, OH 45249
www.samhainpublishing.com

Editing by Heidi Moore
Cover by Kanaxa

First Samhain Publishing, Ltd. electronic publication: April 2012
First Samhain Publishing, Ltd. print publication: March 2013

Dedication

For the readers who loved Nick as much as I did and wanted him to get his own happy-ever-after.

I feel it in my heart
Like a rhythm
Like a curse.
I gotta run to you, babe
I gotta run.

"Gotta Run"
Nick Blackthorne

Chapter One

Plus One.

Nick Blackthorne read the two words written in ornate gold-embossed script again. For the umpteenth time in fact, since receiving the invitation currently in his hand.

Plus One.

The list of viable plus ones he could ask to McKenzie Wood and Aidan Roger's wedding was long and colourful, the stuff of a celebrity mag's fantasy. He was Nick Blackthorne after all, the world's biggest rock star, a man with a reputation for dating and bedding only the most famous and beautiful women on the planet. A gossip-rag journo would have a wet dream over any possible Nick Blackthorne plus one. The thing was, of the bevy of beauties and starlets and award-winning personalities Nick knew would be more than happy to accompany him to Mack and Aidan's wedding, he didn't want to ask any of them.

"Nicky?"

The gruff, deep voice sinking directly into his ears through his headphones made him blink. He lifted his stare from the wedding invitation in his hand to find his record producer looking at him through the studio's glass petition. "Sorry, Walt," he spoke into the mic hanging from the ceiling. "Guess I was wool-gathering."

Walter Winchester, uber-record producer and soulless

mercenary from Hell, gave him a steady look. "Still trying to decide who you're going to take to that wedding? You could take my daughter."

Nick rolled his eyes, shoving the invitation into his jeans' hip pocket. "Your daughter's my agent, Walt, *and* married."

Walter curled his lip. "Yeah, to a gardener."

Nick laughed. "To a world-famous gardener with a client list you'd kill for. I think it's time you accept the fact that your daughter's not a chip off the old block and unlike you, actually *has* a heart."

Walter snorted. "Unlike us both, Blackthorne, although I have to admit you've been a bit soppy since that weekend you spent on that island, thank fucking God. Otherwise I'd be thinking you'd never record another fucking album again." He narrowed his eyes. "What exactly went on at that resort? Whatever it was, there's been sweet fuck-all mention of it in the press."

Nick's heart thumped hard against his breastbone, hard enough he had to wonder if the sound technician sitting beside Walter registered it. As always, the memory of his time at Bandicoot Cove Island Resort made his pulse quicken and his heart fill with warmth. If it wasn't for that weekend, and his time spent with Mack and Aidan, he never would have found the music in his soul again.

If it weren't for Mack and Aidan, who knew what state he'd be in now?

"Nicky?"

He started at Walter's sharp voice, his focus returning to the control room on the other side of the glass partition. The record producer studied him, charcoal-grey eyes narrow, his stare drilling. Nick's bodyguard now stood beside Walter, a worried expression on his face. Over the years in his service,

Aslin Rhodes had evolved from a detached yes-man with muscle to a loyal and honest friend. At times Nick teased him with the title Uncle Aslin, a term the ex-special forces commando pretended to scoff at. Aslin was only two years older than Nick, after all. Today he looked very much the concerned family member—if a somewhat large and menacing one—his black eyebrows drawing together over eyes both sharp and inescapable. He leant forward and activated the communication channel between the control room and recording space where Nick now stood.

"What's up, Nick? Need me to get you anything?" Aslin's voice rumbled, an almost flat timbre Nick thought sounded like distant thunder. Or artillery detonating—quite fitting for an SAS officer, really.

Nick shook his head, offering both Aslin and Walter a wide smile. "Nah, I'm okay. Just trying to remember the words to the next track."

Walter punched the comm. "Well, hurry the fuck up and remember them. For fuck's sake, Nicky, it's only a reworked version of 'Night Whispers'. Surely you can remember the words to the first fucking platinum record you ever wrote?"

Nick blinked. Every muscle in his body coiled. Grew tight. "'Night Whispers'?" The song's title felt like dust on his tongue. He frowned at Walter. "Who said anything about a re-release of 'Night Whispers'? I thought the next song was 'Clouds of Pain'? I didn't agree to recording 'Night—'"

"Surprise. I thought it'd be a nice touch," Walter spoke over him, his teeth flashing behind his lips, his eyes hard as ice and twice as cold. "It's been fifteen years since your first album, Nicky. Since your first international success."

Nick's gut clenched. He swallowed, staring at his record producer. Walter Winchester stared back, his expression set.

The man didn't top Australia's Most Infamous list for nothing—Walter knew "Night Whispers" would make a truckload of dollars with a re-release, especially after Nick's two years of self-imposed recording and performing silence. The predatory, hungry gleam in Walter's eyes almost made Nick laugh. Almost.

If it wasn't for the song Walter wanted him to sing now.

"Nick?" Aslin's soft British accent danced over his ears. "Want me to clear the room?"

Nick's blood pounded in his throat. Words caressed his senses. Lyrics teased him...

And I want to beg but I can't find the words.

And I want to cry but I can't find the tears.

"Shut the fuck up, Rhodes," Walter snapped, his voice a snarl in Nick's headphones. "Nicky doesn't want anything except to sing the fucking song. Right, Nicky?"

Nick closed his eyes, an image of a woman lying on his bed, her hair a golden-red fan around her head as tears like diamonds rested on her cheeks, filling his mind.

And all that's left is the shadow of your heart and the ghost of your smile.

"The song that started it all." Walter chuckled, the sound cold. Triumphant.

And the whispers in the night.

"Thought you'd like to commemorate your new album with a re-release of your first global number one."

And the whispers in the night.

Nick drew a deep breath.

"Night Whispers" was the song he'd written for Lauren. The song that gave him his first simultaneous US, UK and Australian chart topper. The song that said what he'd been too stupid to say when he needed to say it: I choose you.

His first international number one.

Plus One.

The words from the wedding invitation came back to him.
Plus one.

One.

Number one.

He couldn't ignore the significance of that number. His first
number one record was written about a woman who had been
his *number one* everything—friend, love, sexual partner—and
now, here he was, being invited to bring a plus one to Mack and
Aidan's wedding and the only *one* he could think about was the
one he'd sung about all those years ago, the woman who'd
whispered in the night how much she'd loved him, the one he'd
stupidly let go...

Lauren.

He opened his eyes and looked at Walter standing on the
other side of the glass. The producer's capped white teeth
glinted at him like those of a shark about to devour its next
meal, steel-grey eyes just as threatening.

"I've gotta go."

Walter's mouth fell open. "What do you mean, you've—"

Nick didn't hear the rest. He pulled off his headphones,
Walter's incredulous shout nothing but a tinny squeak on the
air as he tossed them onto the nearby padded stool. He gave
Aslin a quick grin, more than happy when the massive man
gave him a grin back before nabbing Walter's right arm in a
tight grip and bending him at a right angle over the control
panel.

Go, his bodyguard mouthed at him.

Nick nodded, a laugh bubbling in his chest at the sight of
Walter Winchester—record producer and soulless mercenary—

desperately trying to free himself from the six-foot-four ex-SAS officer's effortless grip. He gave the grinning technician beside the futilely thrashing Walter a wave and then crossed the room, pulling the wedding invitation from his jeans pocket as he did so.

Plus one.

He knew who he wanted to take to Mack and Aidan's nuptials. Now he needed to find her.

He pulled the soundproof door open and crossed the threshold, the sound of Walter screeching at Aslin to "let me go, you dumb-fuck Pom" making him chuckle some more. After ten years of being Nick's record producer, of interacting with Aslin every time Nick entered a studio, Nick assumed Walter knew better than to resort to insulting the bodyguard's nationality, but apparently not. A solid thud followed the word Pom, a loud *oww* following that.

"Call me a dumb-fuck again," Nick heard Aslin suggest from the control room, his British accent suddenly a whole lot more pronounced despite his menacing chuckle. "Go on, I dare you."

Nick laughed again, the sound utterly joyous. He shook his head, one part of his brain wondering how long it would be before his bodyguard let Walter go, another part wondering just how long it would take to find...

Lauren.

Her name played over his senses, soft and gentle like her, teasing him just like she had all the way through high school.

And just like it had in high school, his body reacted to that tease—his heart thumping harder, his mouth growing dry, his hands growing sweaty.

Nick let out a groan, quickening his pace through the studio's rabbit-warren-like hallways until he was almost running. With a nod at the receptionist perched behind the front desk—a perky little blonde he'd partied with more than once over the years—he pushed hard at the heavy glass doors and stepped out into the crisp Melbourne winter morning.

Walter didn't slam into him from behind. No one stopped him, in fact, which told Nick that Aslin was still keeping the record producer under control. Perfect.

Lifting the collar of his old, battered leather jacket against the cool breeze, he turned and walked toward Collins Street. He'd grab an overnight bag from his suite at the Grand Hyatt, hail a taxi and get his arse to the airport. If he was lucky he'd be able to catch the next flight to...

Nick slowed to a halt, ignoring the chilly wind tugging at his hair and clothes. Fuck. He had no idea where he was going. The last time he'd seen Lauren they were living in a tiny apartment above a delicatessen in Western Sydney fifteen years ago. They'd moved there from their home town so he could be closer to his newly signed agent—a dubious talent manager by the name of Reginald Eggleston who'd promised a naïve twenty-year-old Nick the world. Lauren had enrolled at Sydney University to study teaching and the pair of them had existed in a crammed environment full of laughter and long nights screwing each other senseless. Then came the groupies, the constant fan mail and women of all ages throwing themselves at Nick. The tours around Australia, around the US, the UK, and then the night Lauren said goodbye...

A thick lump settled high in Nick's throat, and he swallowed. What the hell was he thinking? That she would still be in that stingy little shoebox that always stank of salami? That she would be sitting on their second-hand sofa with its squeaky springs and frayed paisley covering, waiting for him to waltz back into her life? Jesus, had she even finished her teacher's degree? He didn't know. Why didn't he know?

Because you're a selfish prick, Nick. Because Lauren didn't want to go where you were going so you cut her loose and went there on your own, fucking every little groupie who spread her thighs for you on the way. Do you really think Lauren Robbins is going to want to even see you again, let alone go to a wedding with you? Fuck, you really don't have a clue about normal life, do you? For all your self-congratulatory gloating over finding yourself again, after learning who you really are after the shit of the last two years of your life, you still think like a fucking rock star—self-centered, self-absorbed and self-important.

The lump in Nick's throat thickened. Choked him. He sucked in a ragged breath, the chill on the air burning his lungs. "Jesus, you're an idiot."

He curled his fingers—starting to sting from the winter breeze—into a fist, the invitation in his right hand crumpling beneath them. What the hell was he thinking? That he would just knock on Lauren's door, smile at her and say, "Heya, babe. I know it's been a while, but fancy coming to a wedding with me in September?"

Yes, that's exactly what he had in mind. And Lauren would take one look at him, swoon into his arms and say, "Oh, Nick, yes."

He shook his head. Rock star. Such a rock star. He'd spent the last sixteen-odd years of his life never being said no to, getting whatever he asked for, whenever he wanted it and then some. Of course, that's *exactly* how he would expect the scene to play out—his way. Hell, she was probably married by now. She was gorgeous and sweet and funny and wonderful. Why wouldn't she be married? He was such a bloody... "Idiot," he muttered again.

Closing his eyes, he scrubbed at his face. What should he do?

Find her. If for no other reason than to...

What?

He didn't know. Say sorry?

Yes.

An image of Lauren filled his mind, her lips parted in a smile as she slid the key into the lock of their newly rented apartment. Their future was so clear-cut then. He would be a famous musician and she would be a successful, well-loved teacher. A happy-ever-after to write songs about. *Their* happy-ever-after.

Opening his eyes, he un-crumpled the wedding invitation in his hands and read the gold embossed script there once again.

Mack and Aidan's wedding. Two people who were meant to be together from the get-go. Two lovers who became a happy-ever-after Nick knew would last forever.

The lump in his throat sank into his chest, growing heavier, almost painful in its pressure. Damn it, he didn't want to take just *anyone* to Mack and Aidan's wedding. He wanted to take Lauren. And if that meant taking Lauren's more-than-likely husband and their more-than-likely brood of adorable children, he would take them too. And afterwards, he'd kiss her cheek, look into her eyes and tell her how monumentally sorry he was for fucking up, for hurting her. And once he did that he'd leave, letting her get on with *her* happy-ever-after. Maybe, if the gods of music and lyrics were nice to him, he'd find a song in the pain he knew his heart would become.

He reached into his back pocket, withdrew his phone and dialed Frankie Winchester.

His agent answered on the second ring, her voice a low, husky laugh. "I just got a very pissed call from my dad, Nick."

Nick snorted. "So Aslin's let him go, I take it?"

"From what I can figure out from Walter's incensed ranting, that walking mountain you call a bodyguard threatened to shove Dad's dick in Dad's throat if he came after you."

"Err...sorry about that."

Frankie laughed again. "Don't apologise. He's my dad and your record producer, but we both know he's a heartless money-hungry prick. Now, tell me why you up and walked out of the first recording-studio session you've had since that miraculous event I like to call Nick's second coming."

Nick chuckled. "That's what you call it, eh?"

"That's what I call it. When I saw the phone footage of you singing "Tropical Sin" at Bandicoot Cove I knew you were back. When I saw that same footage hit over four-hundred million hits on YouTube I knew you weren't just back but reborn. Who is she and where do I send the thank-you flowers?"

Nick's heart slammed hard in his ears. For a moment he thought of playing it cool, just to string Frankie along a bit. She wasn't soulless like her father, but she was just as ruthless and tenacious when she wanted to be. One of the reasons she was such a brilliant agent. Married life had softened her acerbic tongue somewhat, but when it came to her job, she was still brutal. Unfortunately, he didn't have time for messing with Frankie Winchester this morning, even in jest.

He swallowed, knowing what was about to come next. "I need you to find out where Lauren Robbins is."

As he suspected, Frankie was silent. For a good ten seconds. She knew exactly who Lauren Robbins was. In fact, she was one of the few people who truly did. "Is this your heart asking, Nick?" she finally said, all mirth and bite gone from her voice. "Or something foolish like your head?"

"Both, Frankie. I want to ask her to come to a wedding with me."

There was another short silence. "Are you sure you're ready to open that particular closet again?"

Nick drew in a long breath and let it out with a shaky sigh. "Yeah. I am. Nick's second coming isn't finished yet, Frankie. Until I open that closet I can't close it for good, can I?"

He heard his agent chuckle. "Okay. Although something tells me closing the door isn't what you have in mind. Good for you, boyo."

Nick shook his head, smiling. "Married life has turned you into a romantic, Mrs. Harris."

Frankie chuckled once more. "Yeah, yeah, tell anyone and I'll sic my husband onto you. He could bury you under a pile of manure in forty seconds flat. Now, give me a couple of hours. I'll call you back."

She disconnected without a goodbye, leaving Nick grinning in the street. He felt good. Nervous as shit, but good. What had begun as a new chapter of his life two years ago, when he'd not only discovered that he was adopted but also that he had a kid brother, was now becoming *the* chapter. The chapter that would decide where Nick Blackthorne would go next. Here he was, world-famous rock star about to lay his heart on the line to the woman whose heart he'd torn out and cast aside fifteen years ago. He had no idea how it was going to pan out, but he felt good.

Now all he needed was an address.

And the guts to find himself there.

Chapter Two

Twenty-two six-year-olds gazed up at her, some with snotty-noses—it was winter, after all—some with wind-kissed cheeks, all with wide eyes and open mouths. All silent and enrapt. All sitting motionless on the reading rug.

Wombat Stew. Worked every time.

Lauren Robbins turned the page of the classic Australian picture book, revealing a colourful illustration of a dingo stirring an iron pot while the poor wombat watched. Unbeknownst to the dingo, however, the wombat's friends were about to teach him a lesson. Lauren gave her class a sideways grin before effecting a shocked expression, waiting to see who would spot the other animals' plan first.

"'The very clever Dingo stirred and stirred'," she read, letting the singsong quality of the narrative dance through her voice. She watched the children's reaction, her lips curling at the first hint of a comprehension. Thomas Missen was the first. The little boy realised the dingo was going to be without his stew a mere heartbeat earlier than Rachel Jones to his left. As the words of the story rolled off Lauren's tongue, the rest of the class caught up, giggling and squirming with delight as the lucky wombat escaped being devoured by the egotistical dingo thanks to the help of his clever friends.

"Again!" Thomas cried when—the last page read—she

closed the book and placed it gently on her lap, cover down.

"Again!" the rest of the class called out, eyes bright and wide and happy.

She let out a sigh and shook her head. "Alas, my cherubs, the day is almost done. Any minute now the bell will sound and you will all flee to your homes, forgetting all about me and the wombat and the hungry dingo."

"No we won't." As one, all twenty-two students shook their heads emphatically, their expressions part mortified she would suggest such a thing, part frantic the bell would indeed ring before the afternoon ritual was complete and the book read again.

She huffed out another melodramatic sigh, slumping her shoulders and pouting out her bottom lip. "And I shall be left here with a messy room because my sweet, impatient students neglected to tidy their desks and tuck their chairs under their—
"

Before she could finish, the six-year-olds were on their feet, scrambling for their tiny work areas, shoving papers and books and pencils into their respective places and pushing chairs with gusto beneath knee-high tables.

Lauren watched them, unable to contain her smile. As always, their enthusiasm for the simple joys of life—an entertaining book and a soft rug on which to sit—made her happy. The innocent joy of a child. Unlike the unpredictable moodiness of a teenager. The thought drew a grimace and she shook her head. She'd deal with the teenager when she got home. For now, it was her kindergarteners and *Wombat Stew.*

"Please, Miss Robbins—" Thomas was back on the rug, back ram-rod straight, legs perfectly crossed, hands on knees, elbows locked, "—again."

Twenty-one children all but flew to the carpeted area to join him in his plea, all eyes wide and fixed on her, their small bodies squirming with pent-up delight and anticipation.

She cast their desks an exaggerated inspection from her low reading chair, her fingers curled around the edge of the picture book on her lap. "*Well*," she drew out the word, knowing what was coming next.

"Please, Miss Robbins!" the class erupted as one, a jubilant cacophony of young voices. "Please, please, please?"

She rolled her eyes and wriggled her bottom, grinning at them as she made a show of lifting *Wombat Stew* from her lap. "Oh, okay then. One more time, but only because you asked nicely."

Her class giggled, a short burst of laughter that fell to elated silence when she opened the book to page one.

"'One fine day, on the banks of a billabong, a very clever dingo caught a wombat...'"

The rest of the book was listened to with just as much enthusiasm and appreciation as the first two readings, and by the time the bell *did* ring for the day's end, Lauren was more in love with it than before. It was a perfect way to end the day— quiet children hanging on to every word she uttered, an almost tidy room and Saturday and Sunday waiting for her on the other side of the door. As soon as she finished packing everything away, her weekend would begin. She'd take a relaxing walk to her car on the other side of the school to unwind, the cool winter air a refreshing kiss on her skin. The traditional after-work margaritas with Jen would come next, then it was a weekend spent with Josh doing little but watching movies and experimenting with the new fondue thingamabob she'd won in the school's last fund-raising guessing competition. How she knew there were exactly 2,442 M&Ms in old Mr. Bateman's milking bucket was beyond her, but hey, she wasn't going to turn down a thingamabob that gave her an excuse to eat melted chocolate, was she?

Forty minutes after the last child waved goodbye, Lauren collected her bag, a rather beat-up leather satchel someone she refused to think about had given her during a life she *also* refused to think about. She slung the satchel over her shoulder, checked that the class goldfish, SpongeBob, had been given his weekend feed-block and exited her room, closing the door behind her.

The sky had already begun to turn pink with dusk by the time she'd made her way halfway across the small school's smaller playground. Winter played with the leaves and branches of the ancient gum trees standing guard around the grassed area that served as a Stuck-in-the-Mud arena, a marble-playing stadium and, for the older students, a Catch-and-Kiss amphitheater. She lifted her face into the whispering rasp of the breeze, taking a deep breath of the unpolluted afternoon. That she had ended up here, in Murriundah, the parochial country town she'd grown up in five hours away from Sydney, didn't surprise her in the slightest.

Well, not any more. She had to admit, fifteen years ago she'd thought she'd kind of be anywhere else but—

"Hello, Lauren," a deep male voice said behind her.

Lauren squealed. An honest to goodness squeal. At the same exact second she spun on her heel and swung her satchel, weighed down with two textbooks, her uneaten lunch, car keys, half-empty water bottle, twenty-two hand-drawn self-portraits tucked in a sturdy cardboard folder, her purse and her iPad.

The satchel smashed into the temple of the man standing behind her.

There was a solid thud, a surprised *oof*, followed by an even

23

more surprised, "shit that hurt," before the man went down like a bag of bricks, collapsing to the ground in one fluid, graceful drop. No, not just the man, the rock star. The rock star the whole world idolised, the one who'd grown up in this very parochial town with her.

The rock star who'd stolen her heart in that life she refused to think about.

Lauren's mouth fell open. Her pulse turned into a sledgehammer. She stared at the motionless man lying at her feet, refusing to believe what her eyes were telling her. Nick Blackthorne was here in Murriundah, and she'd rendered him unconscious with the very satchel he'd given to her fifteen years ago.

"Oh, no."

The words were a whispered breath. She dropped to her knees, the ground's winter-damp seeping through the linen of her trousers as she reached out with one hand and gave Nick's shoulder a gentle push. "Nick?"

He didn't move.

Oh boy, Lauren, you've KOed the world's biggest rock star.

She shoved him again, a little harder this time. "Nick?"

He didn't make a sound. Not a bloody one.

"Shit."

Her heart slammed into her throat, just as hard as the satchel had hit his head. She licked her lips and brushed a strand of his black hair from his forehead. He was just as gorgeous as always. Older, yes. He was almost thirty-seven after all, but the years looked good on him. So good. In fact, they suited him. When he'd been a teenager, he'd been god-like in his beauty. When he was in his twenties, that god-like beauty had verged on painful to look at. She'd spent many nights lying in the bed they'd shared for a year and a half, gazing at him while he slept, wondering at his perfection, her belly knotting with love, her sex constricting with longing. And then it had become just her bed, Nick nothing but a ghost in her heart.

She'd stopped reading articles about him somewhere in his late twenties, knowing each one would only make her stupid heart ache. But it was impossible to avoid seeing images of him. He kept popping up on the national news. Australia loved one of their own, especially when they'd won a Grammy or Billboard Award, or when they were dating Hollywood royalty or British royalty, something Nick Blackthorne seemed to do on a regular basis. Even worse was the local *Murriundah Herald*, the small newspaper constantly keeping the town aware of their famous "son" and his activities. Those images were hard to escape, and when she had let herself stare at them for longer than a heartbeat, she'd noticed his late twenties and early thirties only elevated his looks to a lived-in sexiness. The tiny seams around his eyes, the lines by his nose, they all heightened what she'd never forgotten—Nick Blackthorne was a sexy, sexy man. And now here he was, unconscious on his side in the Murriundah Public School's muddy playground, looking even sexier than she remembered.

Damn it, what was he doing here? What the hell was he doing back here?

For me?

She frowned, shaking her head at the notion. No. Nick wouldn't be here for her.

Could be. Isn't that what you've dreamed about for the last fifteen years?

Her frown turned into a scowl. No, it bloody well wasn't. She had moved on. She wasn't still the naïve young woman with impossible fantasies and fairy-tale wishes of happy-ever-afters. And if he was here for her—her heart smashed harder into her throat at *that* thought—he could bloody well bugger off. The last thing she wanted was—

He groaned. A barely audible noise deep in his chest.

Lauren started, a tiny yelp slipping from her. "Nick?"

She nudged his shoulder again, but the groan was about it. "Well, at least I know I didn't kill you," she muttered, giving him a glare. He lay there on the cold ground, long, lean body decked out in black jeans, a black shirt and a black leather jacket she knew would cost more than she earned in a month.

Lauren rubbed at her mouth. What was he doing here? And was he alone? Surely he travelled with an entourage? A bodyguard? She'd seen enough paparazzi images of him to know there was usually a hulking great big guy shadowing him wherever he was. Where was *that* guy?

She sat back on her haunches, studying the empty playground around her. There were no massive hulking great big guys running at her, which meant *she* would have to deal with the unconscious Nick.

A tight twisting sensation stirred in the pit of her belly and she bit back a groan. She was not going to get all horny and excited at the idea of dealing with Nick. Besides, there wasn't a hope in hell she could lift him by herself and carry him to her car, even if she wanted to. At five-foot-six and one-hundred-and-thirty pounds wringing-wet, she wasn't exactly the lugging-unconscious-rock-stars-around type even *if* said unconscious rock star had more than once lay full-length atop her in bed, on the living room floor, the kitchen bench, the—

Lauren slapped her hands to her face, killing the utterly insane train of thought. God, was she an idiot? What the hell was she doing thinking about Nick making love to her?

"You a masochist, Lauren Robbins?" she snarled under her breath, grabbing at her satchel/instrument of destruction before digging her phone from its lethal contents.

She turned it on, keying in Jennifer's number. Hopefully, her best friend was sticking with Friday-afternoon tradition and had closed her vet clinic early. Jennifer was used to dealing with heavy, unresponsive animals, being the only vet in the district. Dealing with an unconscious Nick Blackthorne would be a breeze.

"I've got the margaritas chilling in the fridge already," Jennifer Watson said the moment the connection was made, not bothering with any kind of greeting. "Tell Josh you'll be home later than normal tonight."

"I've got a problem, Jen," Lauren answered, trying hard not to let her gaze roam over Nick. Trying but failing, damn it.

"What's up? And if you tell me you're marking school books I'm coming over there to thump you."

"I'm not marking school books, Jen." Lauren rolled her eyes. "Now shut up and listen carefully."

Jennifer made a dramatic *ooh* sound before laughing. "Okay, Miss Robbins, I'm listening. What's your boggle?"

Lauren bit at her bottom lip. "Umm, you know how I told you I once dated Nick Blackthorne?"

Jennifer let out a sharp snort. "You mentioned it in passing years ago and never let me bring up the subject again. Is this a confession? Did you lie to me? Or are you going to tease me some more with tales of your past? Did you also date Hugh Jackman? Guy Pearce? Geoffrey Rush?"

Lauren laughed, rolling her eyes. "No, I didn't. But I *did* date Nick Blackthorne."

"And I'm going to say the same thing I said when you told me before—lucky bitch. Now tell me what's up?"

Lauren took a deep breath. "Well, he's here now."

Silence answered her. For a good twenty seconds or so. Then Jennifer said, "Nick Blackthorne is here?" Her voice, normally calm and laced with mirth, like she knew a really funny joke and was on the verge of sharing it, raised an octave. "In Murriundah?"

Lauren gazed at Nick's face, his stormy-grey eyes shuttered by thick black lashes resting on cheekbones high and strong. A decidedly purplish bruise was beginning to make itself known on the side of his face. "In Murriundah," she answered on a sigh.

Jennifer made a strangled little sound. "And?"

"And I just knocked him unconscious in the school playground."

"What the *fuck*?"

Lauren jerked the phone from her ear.

"What the hell do you mean you just knocked him unconscious?" Jennifer continued, her voice far from calm and loud enough Lauren could hear each word even with the phone nowhere near her ear. "Why? With what? And *why*? Jesus Christ, Robbins, who are you really and what—"

Lauren returned her phone to her ear. "Jenny!" she snapped, "I don't have time right now. I need your help. I can't move Nick by myself and I can't leave him on the ground. He'll catch a cold—"

"A cold?" Jennifer interrupted. "You can't leave him on the ground because he'll catch a cold? How 'bout you can't leave him on the ground because he's Nick Blackthorne?"

Despite herself, Lauren laughed. "Jen, I need you to forget about that for a moment, and by forget, I mean don't tell anyone he's here. I don't know why he is, nor why he's here seemingly without a bodyguard, but I'd rather we not have the whole town suddenly appear on the Murriundah Public School playground until I know *why* he's here, okay?"

"Okay," Jennifer replied, "but can I at least bring my camera?"

"Jen!" Lauren heard her teacher's voice, and the exasperation in it. Her belly knotted tighter. She remembered this emotion all too well—the exasperation at being accosted while out with Nick, of being pushed aside as girls and women—and some men—tried to slip their phone numbers or their underwear into Nick's pockets. "Please," she said. "I need you to be my friend for a moment, not a fan. Okay?"

The question drew silence from Jennifer.

Lauren caught her bottom lip with her teeth. "Please?"

"Sorry," Jennifer said, and Lauren's heart thumped a little harder at the contrition in her voice. "Really, I'm sorry. Of course I can do that. You just threw me for a loop there, teach. I'm calm. I'm cool. Hear how cool I am?"

Lauren chuckled at her best friend's ultra-contained enunciation. "I can hear. Now get your arse here as quickly as you can. And maybe bring a gel ice-pack."

Jennifer burst out laughing. "I can do that too. But on one condition. You tell me everything, little Miss Secrets, and I mean everything. There's no way you're sitting on something like this."

Everything? Lauren swallowed, studying the motionless Nick. No one knew *everything*, not even—

Oh, shit, Josh.

"Can we take him to your house?" she asked, her mouth dry and her blood roaring in her ears.

"Oh, gee, let me think—" Jennifer made a clicking sound, "—can I bring *the* Nick Blackthorne to my house? Golly, I don't know..."

"Jen!" Lauren growled.

Her best friend laughed—back to the same old Jen that Lauren had known for ten years, since the day she and Josh had arrived in Murriundah only to find an injured possum on their new home's front porch. They'd taken the possum to the town's only vet—one Dr. Jennifer Watson, who herself had been in the town for a grand total of five days. Jennifer had babbled the whole time about all sorts of things, from sexing possums to the right playlist for unpacking a house, making Lauren and Josh laugh and the rest was history. The two women had been fast friends since.

Her gaze wandered back to Nick's face, tracing the line of his lips. She remembered the feel of them so very, very easily, as if their caress on her skin had happened only yesterday. His kisses had been sublime, romantic, sweet, hungry, animalistic, reverent...

Had been, Lauren. Had been. Past tense. You need to remember that.

"...in about ten."

Lauren blinked, her cheeks filling with heat as she realized she'd completely tuned out on her friend.

You sure that's why your cheeks are hot? It's nothing to do with the fact you just relived a million kisses from the man before you in a single wonderful, tormenting heartbeat?

"What?" she blurted out, turning her back on Nick. It was safer that way.

"I'll be there in ten minutes. Do you want me to collect Josh on the way?"

"No!"

The word burst from her, sharp and forceful.

"*Okay,*" Jennifer said, and Lauren could see the wheels of her friend's mind ticking over, processing everything she'd learnt so far. Processing and digesting and coming up with theories.

Lauren closed her eyes and dropped her face into her hand. "Just you. I'll give Josh a call from your place."

"Okey dokey, teach. Be there soon."

Jennifer disconnected, leaving Lauren alone.

Not alone. There's an unconscious rock star behind you, remember?

She pulled a face, ignoring the way her pulse fluttered at *that* little fact. Her pulse *and* her pussy.

Tossing her phone aside, she raised her other hand to her face and rubbed. Her pussy. Bloody hell, she was pathetic. Whatever the reason he was here, Nick sure as hell wasn't here to bonk, and she wouldn't let him if he was. She was over him. Had been for fifteen years.

If she were lucky, Nick Blackthorne would leave Murriundah before everyone got all squealy and silly, and she could go back to being over him quick smart. If she were really, really lucky, he'd leave before Josh knew he was even in the town.

What are the odds of that happening?

She snorted. "None."

"You talking to me?" a low, croaky voice asked behind her, "or are you still in the habit of talking to yourself?"

Lauren's heart—way too happily entrenched in her throat—smashed harder, as if trying to escape her all together. She didn't blame it. She'd like to escape herself right now as well. She lifted her head from her hands—slowly—and reached for her satchel.

"You going to brain me with that again?"

Nick's question was uttered with a husky chuckle—his

31

voice still weak and somehow fragile.

That's 'cause you knocked him out, Robbins. And let him lay sprawled on the cold bloody damp ground for the last ten minutes or so.

"Nice bag, by the way," he went on, the words a little stronger. "Who gave it to you?"

She turned, glaring at him. "You did, you idiot."

He laughed—another husky chuckle—as he pushed himself upright. "I know, I know. Just trying to break the ice." He pushed at a clod of dirt stuck to his jacket's lapel before giving her a quick grin. "Although somewhat less violently than you did." He pushed himself to his feet, unfurling to almost his entire six-foot-one frame. And then, to Lauren's horror, his eyes rolled, his cheeks paled and he staggered sideways.

"Hey!" She leapt to her own feet, reaching for him just as he was about to kiss the dirt again. Guilt crashed over her. "Hey, hey." Her hands found his arms, her fingers curling around his biceps, halting his tumble.

He blinked, his full weight hanging in her grip for a second, pulling her forward a step closer to him. Close enough for his scent to thread into her quick intake of breath.

God, he still smells so damn good.

The thought just had time to register in her whirling brain and in her traitorously fluttering sex before Nick's hands came to rest on her hips. Hands that were warm and firm and there, so there.

"Lauren," he murmured.

She looked up into his face, into his glazed eyes. Her lips parted to say something cutting, pithy, witty—God, *anything* would be better than nothing—when he leant toward her, those angry-sky eyes of his growing intense with clarity, and then his mouth was on hers.

Lord, he still kisses...

His tongue dipped past her lips, seeking and finding hers with little resistance. He tasted as good as he had fifteen years ago—toothpaste and coffee and him. He tasted as good. He smelt as good. He felt as good.

A groan vibrated deep in her chest, echoed by Nick's. Her nipples hardened and her pussy throbbed. Her eyes fluttered closed and she snaked her arms around his neck and buried her fingers in his hair...a fraction of a second before his lips slid from her mouth, down her chin and he crumpled to the ground again. Stone-cold unconscious once more.

Chapter Three

Nothing was in focus. Or coloured. Come to think of it, everything was white and fuzzy and bright. Way too bright. And way too fuzzy. And...muffled, like his head was stuffed with iridescent cotton wool.

Nick groaned, squinting and blinking at the brightness. His head hurt. Why did his head hurt? And where was he? Why could he smell disinfectant?

He rubbed at his eyes with his hands, letting out another groan when thick licks of pain lashed through his head. Jesus, what the fuck had happened? Where the hell was he?

Satchel.

Lauren.

The two words floated through his head, disconnected and confusing. Lauren? Lauren Robbins? Satchel? Why was he thinking of Lauren Rob—

It came back to Nick. All of it. In a smashing wave of colour, smell and bone-crunching touch—driving to Murriundah, to the small public school he'd once attended thirty-odd years ago, seeing his old girlfriend walking across the playground carrying the bag he'd given her, trotting up behind her with a nervous smile on his face, his heart thumping, saying her name...

"She hit me," he uttered on a moan, rubbing at his face

some more. "She hit me with her satchel."

"You scared me."

The soft feminine voice stroked over his ears and, eyes flinging open, Nick sat bolt upright.

Pain exploded in his head, sharp and white and blinding. The cotton wool turned to steel wool, making him wince. The fuzziness turned to blurring vertigo, making his stomach lurch, and then everything cleared and he was staring at Lauren Robbins perched on the side of the bed he was stretched out on.

Bed.

Lauren.

Those two words didn't float through his head, disconnected and confusing, they positively *rushed* at each other, their intention undeniable. He was on a bed with Lauren Robbins. A soft bed.

She frowned at him, her deep-auburn eyebrows coming together above eyes a crystalline-blue. "Nick?"

A blur of sensations suddenly swirled through him— Lauren's body pressed to his, her arms around his neck, her lips moving over his as his tongue stroked over hers. A kiss? Had he kissed her? Had she kissed him back? When?

He blinked. A wave of dizziness rolled over him, turning everything fuzzy again. The cotton wool in his head made the air sound like flesh scraping over a mic turned up to maximum. He licked at lips dry and tingling, raking an unsteady hand through his hair. "I feel like shit."

"The life of a rock star?"

He couldn't miss the edge in her voice. Lowering his hand, he gave her a lopsided smile, doing his best to ignore the way his heart thumped harder at the creamy perfection of her skin, the smattering of freckles on her cheeks. God, he'd loved those freckles. "If you mean a life of debauchery and drug use," he said, keeping his own voice relaxed despite the rather enthusiastic blood flow making its way to wholly inappropriate parts of his body given the situation, "you're only half correct. The last time a narcotic and I had anything to do with each other was the time you and I shared a joint behind Mrs. Forester's garden shed."

Lauren's cheeks flushed pink heat and she let out a sigh, rolling her eyes. "Of course you would remember that." She poked a finger at him. "Your father blamed me for that right up to the day your parents moved back to Newcastle."

Nick laughed, the throb in his head echoing the hiccupping beat. "It was your fault. It was your cousin who gave it to us."

"And *your* cousin who ratted us out to your dad." She glared at him, her freckles a darker shade thanks to the blush still tainting her cheeks. "Why I thought sharing a joint with a cop's son was a bright idea is beyond me."

He grinned at her. His heart beat just a little harder, his groin noticing she still looked gorgeous when indignant. "Because you wanted to get in my pants?"

She rolled her eyes again, crossing her arms across her breasts—breasts, he couldn't help but remember, that were heavy and full and divine to fondle and suckle and...

His cock jerked in his jeans. His damn near fully engorged cock. Shit, now was not the time to get an erection.

Huh. Lauren Robbins is in the same room as you. That was once the perfect time to get an erec—

"I didn't want to get into your pants," she grumbled. "You wanted to get into mine."

"Still do."

The confession was out before he could stop it. It hung on the air between them, undeniable, irrefutable and bloody well discommodious. How he felt for Lauren Robbins had no bearing on the situation. It was *not* why he was here. That he wanted to lay her flat on this bed—her bed? It didn't smell like her—and reacquaint himself with her lush, beautiful body held no sway over his actions. That he wanted to lose himself in her full, giving mouth, her round, bountiful breasts, her long, firm thighs, her tight, warm pussy had no influence on his behaviour at all. It couldn't. He was here to ask her to a wedding and tell her he was sorry for breaking her heart. That was it. Nothing else.

And yet your dick is as hard as a bloody pole and your pulse is slamming in your throat. Remember this, Nick? This is the way you used to feel every night—every night—when you were together. Every night when you made love to her. Before you up and left.

"Lauren, I didn't mean to—"

"Why are you here, Nick?" she cut him off with a whisper.

"So, the famous Nick Blackthorne is awake?"

Nick started at the new voice, the new *female* voice. He jerked back from Lauren a little, swinging his stare in the direction of the voice, the throbbing in his head dialing up a notch as he did so.

A tall, willowy woman with hair darker than a moonless midnight and eyes the same inky black stood in the bedroom's open doorway. Her eyebrows were raised, her lips looking for all the world like they were losing a battle with a grin.

"I must admit," she continued, crossing the room to stand beside Lauren, that same almost-grin playing on her lips, "I don't know whether to go all fan-girlie and faint or laugh myself silly Lauren knocked you out with her handbag."

Nick chuckled, giving his temple a bit of a rub. "If I knew one day she was going to whack me in the head with it, I would've given her a clutch purse instead."

The woman raised her eyebrows even higher. "*You* gave it to her?" She burst out laughing, the sound bouncing around the room in unfettered peals of mirth. "Oh, that's priceless."

Nick grinned, even as his head ached. "So was the bag. I bought it for her with the royalties of my first single."

"Really?" The woman plonked down on the bed beside Lauren, sending fresh waves of pain through Nick's head. "That is so romantic."

Lauren let out a snort. "Romantic is calling your girlfriend for her birthday from the other side of the world *without* a woman in the background cooing and gahing your name."

The comment hit Nick like a fist. His grin vanished. He remembered the incident Lauren was referring to all too easily. It had been his second week touring the UK, a naïve twenty-one-year-old thrust into a world of adulation he wasn't equipped to deal with, a second-story hotel room with a window he should have locked, a fan who wouldn't take no for an answer. The woman—twice his age by the looks of her—had thrown herself on stage during that night's performance, screaming Nick's name. Carted off by the concert's hired muscle, she'd promised to come to him later. She'd kept that promise, right in the middle of Nick's eagerly awaited call to Lauren for her nineteenth birthday. Aslin had been employed the next day. Lauren had taken weeks to placate.

Or so Nick had thought. It seemed she hadn't been placated at all.

Maybe you should go now, Nick. She hasn't exactly made you feel welcome.

So why did the memory of a kiss keep teasing him? The memory of Lauren's fingers in his hair, her tongue touching his teeth, his tongue, her breasts crushed to his chest...

His head swum. His cock throbbed.

Had she kissed him? Out on their old school's playground? Somewhere between braining him and him passing out...twice...had she kissed him? And if she had, what did that mean?

"Err..." the new arrival perched beside Lauren said, looking decidedly unsettled.

He gave her a wry smile, pulling himself more upright in an attempt to hide his rather insistent erection. "What Lauren is trying to say is I was a grade-A jerk back then. An innocent, rather clueless grade-A jerk, but a grade-A jerk all the same."

The woman flicked Lauren a sideways glance, as if waiting for her to join the tête-à-tête.

Lauren didn't. She pushed herself to her feet, wiping her hands on her thighs. Thighs, Nick noticed, that still looked amazing in snug pants. "I'm sorry I knocked you out, Nick," she said, looking very much *not* sorry. "But Jennifer here says you're going to be okay, so if you want to tell me where your car is...?"

Nick shot Jennifer a grin. "*You* say I'm okay? Are you a doctor?"

Jennifer grinned back at him. "Vet."

He laughed, his head throbbing in time. "Of course you are." He swung his gaze to Lauren where she stood, a few feet away from the bed, her hands tucked under her armpits, her teeth gnawing on her bottom lip. The urge to climb from the bed—he still didn't know who it belonged to, but something told him it wasn't Lauren's—surged through him. Climb from the bed, walk to Lauren, capture her face with his hands and kiss her senseless.

But he didn't. He may be a rock star to the rest of the world, but right here, right now, he was just the ex-boyfriend who'd turned up unexpectedly, ergo, he had some explaining to do. And some questions to ask.

"Are you married?"

So, not taking the tactful route today, Blackthorne?

He bit back a curse. Okay, the hit on the head obviously had done more damage than he suspected. Like destroying any ability he had to control what was coming out of his mouth.

Lauren gaped at him. Jennifer snorted. "No, she isn't, but she's got a—"

"Another appointment," Lauren burst out, hurrying over to Nick. "So, if you can tell me where your car is?" She curled her fingers around his upper arm, just above his elbow and gave him a gentle tug.

Two things happened at once. Dull pain laced through his head at the shift in position of his upper body and his breath caught at the sudden and altogether vivid memory of Lauren's fingers against his arm in their old school's playground a second before he kissed her.

A heartbeat before she kissed him back.

His gaze locked on hers. "You *did* kiss me."

"You kissed him?" Jennifer squealed.

Lauren's eyes grew wide. "I-I..."

Nick rose to his feet, slowly, until he stood directly before her, their thighs brushing, holding her stare the entire time. "You kissed me," he repeated on a low murmur. "Just like this."

He lowered his head and took her lips with his. They were soft, as he remembered them being. Soft and sweet and warm. He stroked the tip of his tongue over them, an exquisite tension spreading through his body as they parted. Her tongue touched his, hesitant, almost shy. It was enough. Enough to bring their past, their passion, their desire, rushing back to him. He groaned, low and unabashed, and plunged his tongue deeper into her mouth, his hands snaking around her waist to snare her shirt in two tight fistfuls. She whimpered in reply, the sound pushing him over the edge.

With another groan—this one far more aggressive—he yanked her to his body, taking utter possession of her mouth as his hands roamed her back. She fit to his frame with perfection, firm and soft and lush. Nothing had changed. Her body against his ignited a primitive need in him he'd never been able to vocalize, not in song or word, no matter how many times he'd tried. It sparked a want beyond the physical.

He raked his hands up her back and tangled his fingers in her spun-copper hair, shorter than it had been the last time he saw her but no less silken, no less intoxicating with its thick, unrestrained waves.

Lauren moaned, her hips pressing harder to his. White-hot awareness shot through him, a sizzling tension that made his pulse quicken and his balls throb. He plundered her mouth with desperate greed, drinking in her breath, her equally hungry need. This...this... Why had he walked away from this? Was he insane?

She moaned again, her hands sliding up his shirt, slipping beneath his collar. Her skin touched his and there was nothing hesitant about the contact. She splayed her fingers over his shoulders, up the back of his neck and into his hair, pulling him deeper into their kiss. Her tongue mated with his, fierce and demanding. A noise sounded to Nick's left—distant and unimportant—like someone coughing. But he didn't care. Lauren was kissing him. His Lauren. His goddess. She was kissing him and grinding her sex against him and holding him as if she never would let him go again.

Christ, she infused him with heat. With life. Why the fuck had he ever—

"Ahem!"

The word scratched at Nick's senses, loud and filled with laughter. With a gasp, Lauren jerked away from him, staggering back a step as she swung her stare to the smirking woman watching them from the bed. Her cheeks filled with fresh pink, but it was her lips that caught Nick's attention. They were swollen and glistening with his kiss. His cock gave an insistent little twitch in his jeans at the sight. He wanted to kiss her again. Kiss her and hold her and fuck her.

"Guess that clears up my next question."

Jennifer's chuckled statement pulled his stare from Lauren's flushed face. "What question is that?" he asked, struggling to control his voice. And the urge to reach into his jeans and adjust himself. Fuck, he was in pain here, his cock swollen and pumped full of demanding blood and trapped at an odd angle.

The vet raised her eyebrows. "How's your head feeling?"

For a split second Nick thought she was talking about the only head that seemed to matter at that very point in time, the bulbous one on the end of his dick trying to escape his jeans. He blinked, at a loss for words, before rational thought kicked him in the arse and realization dawned. He touched his temple to show her he knew what head she was talking about. "My head's fine, thanks, doc."

"Good," Lauren snapped, *her* voice far from controlled. "Then you can go."

"I don't think so, teach." Jennifer pushed herself from the bed and gave them both a steady look, her black eyes twinkling with barely concealed mirth as she turned to Lauren. "As Mr. Blackthorne's medical practitioner I must insist he stay put for at least twenty-four hours."

"You're not his medical practitioner. You're a vet."

Jennifer made a dismissive sound. "Animal, rock star. All the same thing when burst blood vessels and concussions are involved."

Nick nodded. "I agree. I'm not fit to drive back to Sydney in my condition."

Lauren rolled her eyes. "And what condition is that, Mr. Blackthorne?"

"Horny," Jennifer offered before Nick could say a word.

Lauren snorted. "Deluded, more like it."

Jennifer's eyebrows lifted. "Hey, I just watched you stick your tongue down his throat as eagerly as he stuck his down yours, Miss Robbins, so you can drop the indignant act."

"I—"

But the woman didn't let Lauren finish. "Now if you'll excuse me, I have somewhere else to be."

Lauren's mouth fell open. "No, you don't."

But to Nick's delight, Jennifer ignored her, pivoting on her heel and crossing the bedroom in a few long strides. "Make sure you clean up after yourselves," she threw over her shoulder a second before she walked through the doorway and pulled the door closed behind her.

Nick laughed, even as his balls grew tighter and his cock jerked. He knew if he let Lauren get the chance she would try to deny what had just happened. He wasn't going to give her that chance. Just as she turned back to him, her face set in a glare, her finger raised—no doubt ready to tell him to go to hell—he slid his hand into the hair at the nape of her neck and claimed her mouth once again.

She fought the kiss. For exactly one wild thumping heartbeat. And then she surrendered to what was already in complete control of Nick—pure, undeniable desire. The desire of their past, the desire that had fed them for so long nothing else

43

had mattered.

He worshipped her mouth, her lips, her throat. He scored lines along her jaw, up to her ear, back to her lips. She whimpered nonsensical sounds that filled his cock with fresh want. Whispered words fell from her lips, words that belonged to unfinished sentences like, "This can't... I need... I... You... Please..."

When he slipped his right hand from her hair and covered her breast with it, she sucked in a gasp, her hips pushing to his with an unspoken request. Her nipple pressed at the centre of his palm, hard and insistent. A tremor rocked through her and she let out a hitching breath. "Nick...please."

He knew she was asking him to stop even as she was begging him for more. Her voice wavered, torn with need and confusion. "Don't ask me to stop, Lauren," he groaned against her throat. He could feel her pulse beneath his lips, rapid and strong. "Unless you really want me to walk away, right now, don't ask me to stop."

"Nick," she choked, her hips rolling against his. "We can't do this..."

He lifted his head, his gaze roaming her face. Her ragged breath caressed his lips, her eyes were closed, her face etched with pleasure. Pleasure he'd given to her with just a kiss. A kiss.

"Are you with someone, Lauren?" His gut churned, his voice cracking on the question. He had to ask. No matter how much he hated the expected answer. "Is that why you want me to stop? Is that why you're fighting so hard to deny what's so very undeniable? If you are, I'll stop. I'll stop right now." He swallowed, clenched his teeth. "Just tell me if you are."

Her eyes squeezed more tightly shut. Her teeth caught her bottom lip. She didn't answer.

His stomach knotted. His cock pulsed. She was so soft in his arms, against his body. Her heat was so close to his, her breasts so full, her lips so sweet. Fuck, he wanted her. More than he could comprehend. Wanted to bury himself in her heat and give her everything he was.

Weren't you here only to ask a question?

He was. And he had. And she hadn't said yes.

"Let me make love to you, Lauren." He pressed his mouth to the base of her throat, stroking the tip of his tongue into the shallow dip there. "Let me show you what we both once had."

He slipped his hand under her shirt, his head swimming at the velvet warmth of her skin. His fingers danced over her ribcage before brushing the under-swell of her breast. Lace rasped his fingertips and an image of Lauren in her underwear from a lifetime ago filled his head, making it swim some more. She'd always loved beautiful underwear—lacey bras and knickers, usually white or the deepest burgundy. What colour was she wearing today?

His heart slammed faster at the thought and, unable to stop himself, he shifted his arm, bunching up her shirt to reveal that which his hand so desperately wanted to possess.

"Oh, babe," he groaned, his stare falling on a cherry-red bra perfectly cupping her breast. Her nipple strained at the delicate lace, drawing his attention and making his breath quicken. "You are as beautiful as I remember."

He bent and took her nipple in his mouth, rolling its taut form under his tongue before suckling on it hard through the lace.

"Nick," Lauren raked her nails over his shoulders, her hips bucking forward. He pressed his free hand to the small of her back, holding her still as he drew on her breast. She whimpered, clinging to him, those wordless sounds slipping

45

from her again. Wordless sounds that grew to raw pleas. "Oh, Nick, that feels so good. So good..."

He laved her nipple, caught it between his teeth and flicked his tongue over it. She arched in his arms, one long leg wrapping around the back of his thigh. His blood roared through his veins, in his ears at the warmth of her sex, her pussy, so close to his groin. It shoved him dangerously close to the edge.

"Fuck me," he ground out against her breast, raking his hand down to her arse to cup her left cheek, "I'm about five minutes away from—"

She reached up and yanked her bra aside, freeing her nipple of the concealing lace, and the rest of his sentence was lost to him.

He latched onto the taut point of flesh, drawing it into his mouth with hungry need. Lauren moaned and arched into him, stroking her heat against the length of his erection through their clothes, her nails digging into the backs of his shoulders. A disconnected part of his mind wondered where his leather jacket had gone. A far more involved part pointed out it didn't fucking matter. Lauren Robbins was in his arms. Who the fuck cared about a jacket?

He scooped her breast, now completely released of her bra, deeper into his palm, massaging its beautiful weight as he feasted on her nipple. With every suck and nip, she whimpered, thrusting her pussy harder to his cock. His straining, throbbing cock.

Ah, Christ, he was close to coming.

It was always this way with Lauren, Nick. You lost control every time she touched you. Lost control and lost yourself in her heat, her smell, her taste...

The thought seared into him, hot and powerful. Every song

he'd ever written was about her, every rhyme forged by what they'd had and what he'd walked away from.

And now here he was, her flesh in his mouth, her nipple under his tongue, her pleasure turning the air musky.

Christ, he wanted to be inside her.

He straightened from her breast, grazing her chin and mouth with his lips before dragging his thumb over her nipple. "Let me make love to you, Lauren. Right now."

She opened her eyes, gazing up at him through heavy lids. "Nick..."

His name fell from her lips, part supplication, part request.

Without another second wasting time, he hauled her off her feet, threw her onto the bed and crushed her to the mattress with his body. He captured her lips with his, his kiss as savage as his lust. His head roared, the pain of his concussion insignificant to the dire need, the concentrated pleasure consuming him. She writhed beneath him, her hands raking over his back, her sex grinding to his erection.

Fuck, it felt so good. So good. So potent and raw. It was as if they were two horny teenagers all over again, discovering each other with the full force of hormonal need. The first time he'd possessed her they'd been just that, barely legal and so fucking on fire he'd hardly stroked into her tightness once before losing his load. The second time—fifteen minutes later—had been just as hot, just as powerful. She'd cried out his name both times, begged him for more. Told him she loved him.

And he'd buried his face in her neck, one hand on her breast, one hand knotted in the sheet of her single bed, his cock sheathed inside her wet heat, and told her he loved her too, would love her forever.

Fuck, how had he let it all go so wrong?

Fix it now. Give her everything you should have the last

fifteen years. Make her remember what it was like. Make her cry your name. Make her plead for more. Make her love you again.

He tore away from the kiss, hooked his hands under the hemline of her shirt and yanked it up over her head before she could utter a sound. Her breasts jiggled with the force of his disrobing, her nipples hard points—one still trapped by the cup of her bra, one revealed to his gaze. With a growl, he ripped the skimpy undergarment apart, Lauren's squeal making his cock jerk in his jeans.

He captured first one nipple and then the other with his mouth, suckling with ravenous want. She moaned and twisted beneath him, her fingers scraping at his shoulders. With another growl, he snatched her wrists and pinned them to the bed beside her as he thoroughly sucked on her breasts. She made sounds, sweet sounds, wordless sounds, her legs wrapping around his thighs, pulling him harder to her sex.

Nick's heart punched faster, driving eager blood into his shaft. His pulse thumped in his ears, a rapid beat echoed by the throb in his groin. He dragged his mouth over her smooth flesh, nipping at the under swell of her breasts with increasing urgency before sliding his tongue and lips down the line of her belly to the indent of her navel.

As she always did, she hissed in a sharp breath. Lauren's belly button was an erogenous zone and Nick wasted no time lashing it with feverish attention. He circled its circumference with the tip of his tongue, painted its shallow depths with broad strokes. She bucked each time, a hiccupping, "oh, yes, yes," accompanying each physical reaction to his tongue's caress.

When he felt the muscles in her thighs begin to quiver, when he felt a tremble work through her body, he moved lower. How could he not when he pulled Lauren's scent into his being with every breath he took? He could taste her pleasure, her need on the air, a perfume so familiar to him that for a dizzying moment he almost believed he'd never been without it.

His chin nudged the waistline of her trousers. He released her wrists and fumbled with her fly, lifting his head from her belly only long enough to watch his hands slide her snug charcoal pants down over her hips.

His heart slammed into his throat. His mouth went dry. "Oh, babe..."

She lay before him, nothing covering her from his gaze but a pair of tiny red lace knickers.

Lace of her heat, slips into my soul, keeps her from me forever and I grow

The lyrics from a song he'd written a decade ago whispered through his mind, a song about a woman called "Heartbreak". A tormented song. A tortured song.

He didn't want to listen to them, think about them. He wanted...

"To taste your honey on my tongue," he murmured, a second before he pressed his palms to Lauren's inner thighs, spread her legs wide and lowered his head to her pussy.

"Oh, Nick!"

She moaned his name as his tongue stroked her folds through the lace of her undies, her hips thrusting upward to meet his touch. She sucked in a ragged breath, shoving her hips higher as he flicked at her clitoris.

The lace rubbed at his tongue and he growled, snagging the crotch of her knickers with a finger and yanking it aside. The scent of her pleasure filled his breath instantly. His cock swelled harder at the subtle musk. "You taste as good as I remember, babe." He spoke against her inner thigh, his lips brushing her skin as he ran the pad of his thumb over her wet seam. "I want more."

He slipped his thumb into her pussy, lapping at her clit as

49

she bucked into his penetration. She called out his name, louder this time, her hands grabbing at the bed's duvet. He wriggled his thumb deeper, sucking the nub of her clit into his mouth, laving it over and over again with his tongue.

"Nick." Lauren's gasps turned his name to a breathless pant. "Nick, I...I'm..."

"Come for me, baby," he urged against her sex, withdrawing his thumb long enough to dip his tongue inside her damp folds. "I want to fucking drown in your orgasm."

He stabbed his tongue and his thumb back into her heat, wriggling both before driving his thumb deeper and lashing her clit with his tongue. Her moans grew louder, her hips bucked higher, harder. His dick ached in his jeans, a rod of steel ready to burst. As soon as Lauren came, as soon as he brought her to climax with his mouth, he would sink his length into her dripping, clenching sex. As soon as she came...

He caught her clit with his teeth, nipped once and then suckled.

"Fuck!" Lauren's scream rent the air, the word long and hitching. "Oh fuck, yes, yes."

Her cream flowed from her, painting Nick's lips and chin, and still he worshipped her sex. Still he suckled and bit and lapped, all the while releasing his fly with one shaky hand. He freed his cock of its denim prison, smearing his pre-come over its bulbous head, his mouth full of Lauren, his mind full of pleasure, his heart full of—

Someone started singing "Livin' on a Prayer" from beside the bed. Someone *not* Jon Bon Jovi.

"Shit!" Lauren yelped, her voice high, panicked. "Shit, shit, shit!"

She scurried backward, her heels bunching up the duvet, her feet smacking into Nick's shoulders. He jerked upright, staring at her, his heart smashing into his throat at the abject horror etched on her face.

"Lauren?" He made to crawl after her, but she shook her head, staring at him for a split second, eyes wide, face pale, before lurching sideways and snatching at her satchel sitting on the bedside table.

"Livin' on a Prayer" grew louder as she pulled a slim white iPhone from the satchel's belly and swiped her finger over its screen. Nick caught a glimpse of an image of someone with dark hair and a wide grin, a *male* someone, and then Lauren rammed the phone to her ear, her back turned to him, her spine ramrod straight.

He stared at her back, at the bra strap still dangling from her shoulders, at the tousled curtain of her hair caressing her shoulder blades. His pulse thumped fast in his neck, his cock.

"Hey, Josh," he heard her say, her voice almost, *almost* controlled, and his mouth went dry. "I'm sorry, honey, I meant to call."

Chapter Four

"Yeah, yeah," Josh chuckled in her ear, and Lauren closed her eyes, fighting the need to slump into a ball and cry. "Sure you did, Mum. Any chance you're going to be home for dinner tonight? I mean it *is* after six after all."

Lauren's eyes flung open. She looked at her watch, a loud thump-thump pounding in her ears.

It's your heart, Lauren. Your heart. Pounding so hard because your ex made you forget your son. God, how could you let Nick Blackthorne make you forget about—

"Mum?"

She started, blinking at Josh's voice. "*Are* you going to be home for dinner?" he went on. "I mean, if you're planning on staying longer at Jennifer's than normal can I go over to Rhys'? He's got the new version of Rock Band and we thought we could—"

"I'll be home for dinner, Josh," she cut him off, gripping her phone tighter. She could feel Nick's stare on her back, her naked back. She looked around for her clothes, an unsettled knot twisting in her belly. God, she was naked. He'd managed to get her naked all of about ten seconds after regaining consciousness. Naked and flat on her back on Jennifer's bed. Did she have no shame? No sanity? Was she truly that pathetic? That easy?

She heard Nick move behind her, a soft rustling of material followed by the softer sounds of his footfalls. She tensed, waiting for his touch, her pussy constricting. Instead, his arm extended over her shoulder, her shirt and trousers bunched together in his hand. There was no other contact, no other touch of his body to hers.

Before she could stop herself, she shot him a quick look, her pulse leaping faster in her throat at the expression on his face. It was lost. Tormented.

Without a word, she took her offered clothes, his stare holding her motionless for a moment before she tore her gaze away. Damn it, what did *he* have to feel all tormented about? She was the one who'd had her heart ripped out. She was the one who'd spent the last fifteen years of her life aching for a future long denied her. Not Nick. Nick was the one who'd up and left. The one who'd chosen the life of a rock star over her.

She clutched her clothes to her churning stomach. She needed to be away from him. Now. It was too difficult to think clearly with him near her.

"Josh," she said, interrupting her teenage son's obviously well-considered argument for why he could go to his best friend's house—an argument that consisted mainly of Mrs. McDowell's *awesome* cooking, no homework, Rhys' Wii and Josh's burning desire to reach professional level on Rock Band. "I won't be long. I've just got to get some trouble out of the road and then I'll be home. I'll grab some fish and chips on the way, okay?"

"Then can I head over to Rhys'?"

She should have been angry at Josh's persistence. Instead, she was angry over Nick's presence and the moronic effect it was having on her intelligence.

"I'll be home soon, hon," she said, refusing to answer her

son's question. It wasn't that she didn't want Josh to go to Rhys', but did he have to play Rock Band? Did he have to be so good at it? Did he have to sound so much like his father when he sang?

The last question sliced at her tenuous calm and, squeezing her eyes shut, she disconnected the call and pressed the smartphone's screen to her forehead. The glass was cool on her flushed skin, highlighting just how flustered she was.

Huh. Don't you think standing in nothing but your undies while Nick waits behind you highlights it enough? Or how 'bout the fact that, despite how insane you know the situation is, you want nothing more than for him to close the distance between you both, slide his arms around your waist and begin to seduce you all over again? Like he used to way back when?

"Lauren?"

She didn't open her eyes at his voice. Nor did she turn.

"Lauren, I think you need to tell me who Josh is."

"No, I don't."

"Yes, you do. If he's your husband, I need to know. If he's your boyfriend...I need to know how serious you are."

Lauren laughed. She couldn't help herself. Shaking her head, she opened her eyes and did up her bra, forgoing the usual readjustment of breasts in favour of shoving her arms into her shirtsleeves and covering up her bare torso as quickly as possible. "How serious I am?" she shot over her shoulder. "About Josh? Very serious. About you leaving ASAP? Even more so."

"Lauren, I didn't mean—"

She saw red. The second those words left Nick's lips she saw red. Saw it. Felt it. She spun to face him, fists clenched, jaw bunched. "Yes, you did, Nick." She glared at him, a dull throb in her temple. "As always, it didn't matter what anyone else wanted, you got what *you* wanted. Well, bravo for you, Mr. Blackthorne. You just proved that you still have an effect on my body. Aren't you clever? But you also proved you haven't changed a bit since you left me fifteen years ago. The arrogant, self-centred rock star is still in existence, though why I thought it would be any different is beyond me. So here's a newsflash for you, Nicky. I don't want you touching me again. I don't want you touching me, I don't want you near me and I don't want you talking to me. Please go away and be famous and fawned over elsewhere."

The tirade finished as abruptly as it started, but it left her spent. She closed her eyes against the sight of Nick, standing but a few feet away from her, his face as indelible on *her* existence as a brand on her soul. For all her postulating and carrying on about how she was over him, all it had taken was one kiss—one kiss—and she was his again. To do with what he wanted.

She hated him. For what he'd done to her fifteen years ago. For what he'd done to her just now.

"Believe it or not, I didn't come here to make you angry."

His voice played over her senses, low and deep and husky. It had never ceased to turn her on, Nick's voice. When he sang to her, which he had done often in the early years of their relationship, his voice had been all the foreplay she'd needed. Now, try as much as she did to stop it, her body reacted. Her heart quickened, her nipples pinched tight. His was a voice of sin and pleasure. The voice with the power of the Pied Piper's proverbial flute—except instead of entrancing children, Nick Blackthorne's voice seduced women.

"Why *did* you come here, Nick?" she asked. "Was it to prove something?"

"No."

The single-word answer was so haunted she opened her eyes and looked at him. Her pulse slammed into her throat. That same tormented expression etched his face, but whereas on another man it would make his visage appear wretched, on Nick it just made him look all the more achingly gorgeous—the tortured musical genius, a man ruled by the songs in his soul. Except he wasn't. Lauren knew that. He was ruled by his prick and his ego.

Is he still though? Have you ever seen him look so...lost?

She ground her teeth, folding her arms across her chest and fixing him with a steady stare. "Why did you come here?"

He met her gaze with his own unwavering stare. "I came to say sorry."

Lauren wanted to laugh. She wanted to scoff in his face. She couldn't. Her heart was hurting too much to do that. She licked her lips, her mouth dry. "I don't believe you."

Nick didn't flinch. "It's true. I came to say sorry and to ask you to a wedding."

Lauren blinked. Okay, she hadn't seen that one coming. "A wedding?"

Nick laughed, a self-deprecating snort she'd never heard from him before. It did unsettling things to her stomach.

"It's stupid, I know, but I received an invitation from this amazing couple I met a few months ago, a couple who pretty much saved my life, and the only person in the entire would I can think of who I want to share their special day with is you."

A lump filled Lauren's throat. Thick and fast and choking. She swallowed, but it didn't go away. Nor did Nick suddenly grow two heads. Surely that's what was meant to happen now, wasn't it? Surely this had to be some surreal dream she was in? Nick appearing out of the blue, rendering her defenseless against him with a single kiss and then asking her to a wedding? "A wedding?" she repeated.

He shrugged, a lop-sided smile pulling at his lips. "I'll admit this hasn't gone *exactly* as I planned, but then you always did throw my plans into wild loops, Lauren Robbins."

She held up a finger, giving him a narrowed-eyed scowl. "Don't."

He paused for a second. "Who is Josh, Lauren? I need to know, because I have to tell you something here and now and your answer will greatly impact on just how I go about doing that."

"What do you have to tell me?"

He shook his head. "Who's Josh? Is he your boyfriend?"

Lauren lifted her chin. "If he was? Would you go away then? Leave Murriundah?"

His smile grew more crooked. "No."

"So what difference does it make if he *is* my boyfriend?"

Nick took a step toward hers. "The difference is whether I have to compete with someone or not?"

Lauren's heart slammed harder into her already tight throat. "Compete?"

"For you, Lauren." His grey eyes seemed to glint, as if the hottest of fires suddenly burned in their depths. "I came back to say sorry for fucking up, sorry for walking away from you, from us, sorry for tearing out your heart. I came back to apologise and invite you to a wedding. To share a moment of pure happiness with the only person I have ever been truly happy with, and then you kissed me."

She stared at him. "And?" The word was barely a whispered breath.

"And then you asked for more, and I knew I had more to give you. So much more. I *have* more to give you, Lauren. I have fifteen years of more to give you, if you'll let me, and then a whole lot more."

"No." She shook her head. The ridiculousness of the situation struck her. Here she was standing in her best friend's bedroom wearing only a shirt and underpants as the world's biggest rock star told her quite clearly he wanted her. Again. The world's biggest rock star who could have anyone he wanted, who had women and men throw themselves at him on a daily basis, wanted her.

Say yes.

She shook her head again. "No."

"No you won't let me, or no, you won't tell me who Josh is."

"Both."

He took another step toward her. "Lauren, please."

She stared at him, eyebrows knotting. "Nick, do you have any idea what you did to me fifteen years ago?"

"I think I do. And I want to show you how fucking sorry I am."

"I can't let you do that." She caught her bottom lip with her teeth, hugging herself. "I barely survived the last time you left. Now, it's not just..." She bit on her lip again. "I'm just a school teacher in a small town that doesn't have a single set of traffic lights, and I like that. You're Nick Blackthorne. You date royalty and fly in private jets and have women send you their worn underwear. You're talking about competing, Nick? *I* can't compete with *that*. I can't and I won't. It's not fair to me, and it's not fair to Josh."

Nick's eyes flared that same black heat. "He's a lucky guy, this Josh."

Lauren swallowed. "I like to think so."

"But tell me, Lauren," he murmured. "Does he make you

feel like this?" He destroyed the distance between them in one step to capture her mouth with his.

The kiss was deep and thorough and utterly possessive. It claimed her lips and rendered her knees weak. His hands cupped her face, his fingertips coming to rest on her temples, his thumbs stroking her cheekbones. His tongue delved into her mouth, seeking hers. Finding it, mating with it. She wanted to stop him, she knew she should—it was insane to let him kiss her like this—but the second the notion of pulling away entered her mind it was washed away by the waves of desire and need Nick's kiss sent surging through her.

She moaned, surrendering herself to that desire. For a moment, just a moment. Surely she could allow herself one more moment?

Nick moaned back, a raw sound so full of want her head swum. His heat seeped into her, his body hard and lean against her. So hard. All of him.

She shifted, rolling her hips. His erection pressed to her belly, and not for the first time in her life of being kissed by him, she wished she was taller. She wished she was his height so her sex could align with his. She needed to feel its long, thick length on her mons. Just for one moment...

"Fuck, I love kissing you." Nick's groan, uttered against her lips, sent ripples of tight heat into her core. "It's like kissing a horny angel."

His tongue swiped over hers before she could respond. Or maybe she did? Maybe the whimper in her throat and the thrust of her hips harder to his body was her response? She wasn't sure anymore. Wasn't even sure what she'd been doing before this kiss. Her mind didn't seem to be hers anymore. It was lost to the pleasure welling inside her. All due to Nick's lips, Nick's tongue, Nick's kiss. Her blood roared in her ears and her pussy throbbed. She slid her hands up his torso, the sculpted muscles beneath her palms tensing at her touch. She liked that. Liked the effect she had on him. She skimmed her fingertips over his nipples, her sex squeezing as they puckered into tighter points under the material of his shirt.

His shirt. Lord, why hadn't she removed his shirt along with his jacket? Just to be sure he hadn't been bruised when he hit the ground back at school? If she'd removed his shirt her skin could be touching his skin now. In fact, she should remove her own shirt. Share her body heat with him. Let her warmth heal him. Let her body soothe the pain she'd caused him. It was only right.

She tried to pull away, tried to disengage herself from the kiss. The need to strip naked was too powerful to ignore, but Nick wouldn't let her. His hands raked down her back, his arms cinching around her, as if he feared she was going somewhere. Ha! She wasn't going anywhere. Why would she, when Nick was kissing her with such ruthless abandon and greed? When his erection ground against her belly, an undeniable testament to his desire for her? She moaned again, her innermost muscles clenching, wanting that which her body and her heart remembered all too easily—Nick inside her, possessing her. Filling her. Fucking her.

Making love to her.

Like he used to.

Used to.

The thought slipped through the rising pleasure consuming her mind. Used to. Past tense. There was a reason for that. He'd left her. For something else. For the groupies, the starlets.

She tore her lips from his, turning her head away. She had to stop this, fight it.

Nick's fingers found her chin, returning her face to his, at once determined and refusing argument. His mouth captured hers again, his tongue and lips growing fierce. Arrogant.

Fresh pleasure crashed through Lauren. How was she to resist this? No one had ever kissed her like Nick, with such single-minded purpose and hunger. With a hunger that made her feel worshipped and sensual and wanton and desired beyond reason.

No one else had ever made her ache for more like Nick. No one had ever made her very soul sing.

Oh Lord, she was still in love with him. Still in love with the man who'd broken her heart and *killed* the song in her soul.

A chill razed through the heady pleasure trying to consume her. She stiffened, her stupid, foolish heart leaping into her throat, her intoxicated brain finally catching up with her sanity. She couldn't do this. She couldn't do this again. It was no good for her. No good for Josh. No good for anyone.

She flattened her palms on Nick's chest and shoved. Hard. Hard enough to force him back a stumbling step. He stared at her, chest heaving, eyes smoldering. He looked gorgeous and sexual and dangerous. Oh fuck, if he reached for her again...

"No," she croaked, shaking her head. "I can't."

"I bet Josh doesn't kiss you like that, Lauren," he said, his voice as strained as her own. He pulled a ragged breath, his eyes half-lidded, his pupils dilated. "Tell me he does and I'll walk away right now, but I'll know if you're lying. I always did. I don't want to compete for you, babe, but I will. I will show you what this Josh can't give you, I will reawaken the pleasure I gave you all those years ago until you can't think of anyone else but me. Until you forget all about Josh and let me make you mine again."

Hot, tight tension speared into Lauren's core at Nick's statement. Her sex contracted, grew wet. Her breath caught at the naked desire in his eyes.

Her chest squeezed at the arrogant conceit of his words. Nick the rock star. The man used to getting exactly what he wanted. Damn him.

She clenched her jaw, tilting her chin to fix him with an unwavering glare. "I will never forget about Josh, Nick Blackthorne. I'll forget about you the minute you walk away from me—again—like I did fifteen years ago, but I will never forget about Josh. Ever. And you'll never, ever compete with him."

Nick's eyes flared grey fire. "I beg to differ. And by the smell of your pleasure on the air, so does your body."

Lauren balled her hands into fists. "You will never *compete* with him."

"And why not?"

"Because he's my son. Now leave me the fuck alone."

A calm stillness fell over Nick. His nostrils flared again. His Adam's apple slid up and down his throat. "You *do* have children."

His voice registered his shock. Lauren nodded, wishing she was anywhere else but here. "One. A son. I'm thirty-four, Nick. My life continued after you left. What? Did you think I'd still be pining away for you after all these years?"

He didn't say anything. He didn't even blink. She let out a disgusted snort. If only he knew the truth of that last question. The pain of it. "That changes everything, doesn't it, Nick? Making me 'yours' again isn't so simple when there's a kid on the scene. Kinda brings along a whole lot of extra baggage, doesn't it?"

Still, he didn't say anything. But his eyes never left her face.

"Now, if you'll excuse me, I have to go. Dinner time and all."

"Where's his dad?"

Lauren forced a dismissive laugh from her throat. "Is that any real concern of yours?"

"It is. He's been inside you. I hate him."

A deep, hot pain slowly sank into Lauren's soul. "I hate him too, Nick," she said, unable to keep the torment from her voice. "And I'm one-hundred percent certain you've been inside more than one woman since me, so you don't really have any grounds for being so incensed, do you?"

"Who *is* the father?"

Lauren's chest squeezed. She drove her nails into her palms, her mouth dry. "Someone I knew once."

"Where is he? Here? In Murriundah?"

"I don't have to tell you that."

"So he is then?"

Lauren swallowed. "I didn't say that."

"You didn't have to."

She let out a ragged sigh. She wasn't up to this. Not now. It was too much. "Can you just go please, Nick? I need to go home and give my son his dinner, make sure he's done his homework and mark some schoolwork. That's my life now. You need to go jet off somewhere, sing on a stage, sign some autographs, sleep with a supermodel. That's *your* life. You may be able to make me melt with your kisses—and you *do*, Nick, I can't deny that—but my heart doesn't belong to you anymore. You can't touch it. The guy who *once* could do that with his songs and his kisses left me a long time ago. Now it belongs to a different boy, one who is waiting at home for fish and chips, who rarely gives me a kiss and will most likely pick a DVD about robot trucks to watch on the telly tonight. And you know what? I don't want it any other way."

Nick stood motionless. His gaze held her just as still. She wanted him to say something. She wanted him to say, "Okay, Lauren. I'm going." She wanted him to say sorry.

"How old is he? Your son?"

Lauren swallowed, her pulse thumping so hard in her throat it was painful. It was the question she hadn't wanted Nick to ask. "He's a teenager," she answered, fighting to keep her voice level. "A hungry teenager. Teenagers are always hungry. Must be the hormones. Now, as I said, I have to go home and feed him. Can't stay around and chat anymore. Sorry."

Nick's Adam's apple jerked in his throat.

She drove her nails harder into her palms. "It was nice to see you again, but if you're not leaving, I will. Just lock the door on your way out, okay? Murriundah isn't quite the same town it was when we were growing up."

"How old is your son, Lauren?"

The question was level. Steady. Nick didn't move. Just stood before her, smolderingly sexy, achingly gorgeous and ridiculously famous. Oh God, she didn't want to answer him. She didn't.

But you have to. You know that, right? He won't leave until you do.

"He's a teenager," Nick said, his gaze pinning her to the spot, his expression unreadable, "so what? Thirteen? Fourteen? Can't be older than that."

Lauren swallowed. Her breath caught in her throat. She stared at him, wanting to flee from the room, wanting to run as far away as she could. Unable to take a step. Unable to stop Nick's train of thought.

Oh no. No.

"Can't be fifteen," he went on, "'cause that would make

him..." His voice faded away. His eyes widened.

Her stomach rolled.

"How old is Josh, Lauren? You hate his father. His father's not on the scene. The only piece to the puzzle I don't have is Josh's age."

"There's no puzzle," she said, but even to her ears the words sounded hollow. "He's a teenager, Nick. Stop looking for something that isn't there."

His nostrils flared. "Isn't it?"

A sour taste filled the back of Lauren's throat. "Jesus, you and your ego. Don't you think if you were the father I would have tapped your sizeable income by now? Let the world know *the* Nick Blackthorne has a son? Raising him would be a whole lot easier with a billionaire father, that's for certain." She shook her head. "And if he *was* yours, you gave up the right to anything in my life the night you walked away from it."

Her stomach churned again. She felt sick. Sick and sorry and so goddamn lost.

"That's not fair, Lauren."

"Neither is throwing what we had aside for a horde of groupies." She closed her eyes, letting out a trembling breath. What happened to a quick drink with Jennifer this evening, followed by a weekend relaxing with Josh? How had she found herself skirting such a gaping, surreal chasm so quickly? How had she gone from laughing through *Wombat Stew* without a care in the world to being on the edge of a mental breakdown in one afternoon? How had this happened? And whose fault was it?

Yours? For not telling Nick fifteen years ago what he deserved to know?

She opened her eyes and gave Nick a level look. "I'm going. Please don't follow me." She snatched up her trousers from where they had fallen to the floor during their last kiss and shoved her legs into them, refusing to look at him as she did so. "I'm sure if you leave now you'll get back to Sydney before midnight. Drive safely."

"Lauren," he began, but she ignored him. She had to. As hard as it was, she ignored him. She strode from Jennifer's bedroom, through her best friend's home, out the front door. The winter night air wrapped around her instantly, turning her flesh to goosebumps and her nipples to aching points of flesh. And even as her traitorous mind reminded her how wonderful Nick's lips felt wrapped around those nipples, she walked on, leaving Nick standing on Jennifer's front porch, his stare on her retreating back like a caress she longed to succumb to. She walked to her car, climbed in and drove away. He didn't follow, just as she'd asked.

And it wasn't until she was unlocking her front door, a bag of hot fish and chips from Murriundah's only take-away café hanging from her fingers that she allowed herself the weakness to think of him again, and even then, it was only to wonder how he'd found her in Murriundah to begin with.

"Doesn't matter," she grumbled. "As long as he's not here when the sun comes up."

"Finally!" Josh yelled from the living room, his voice a deep baritone as smooth as silk. "I'm starving!"

She heard his feet—already an enormous size eleven—thump on the floor and then Josh was in the kitchen with her, complaining about how hungry he was as he tore open the bag of food and stuffed a hot chip into his mouth, his grin just like his father's, his eyes even more so.

Lauren's chest squeezed tight. Damn it. How was she to ignore Nick Blackthorne in her life when all she had to do was look at her fifteen-year old son to see him?

Chapter Five

Nick watched the night swallow Lauren's beat-up old Honda Civic, the taillights fading to two dull red spots in the darkness before disappearing completely. He dragged his hands through his hair, ignoring the chilling winter air turning his flesh to goosebumps. He didn't know what surprised him the most—that Lauren still drove the same car she had fifteen years ago, or that he wasn't going after her.

He wasn't going after her. Shit, was he actually going to let her drive away? After dropping a bombshell like that? A son? A teenage son?

He swallowed, scraping his nails through his hair again. A dull weight sat on his chest. His breath puffed from him in balls of white mist and his gut felt like it was one big, knotted mess. Added to that, an angry pain throbbed where Lauren had smacked his head with her satchel, making each blink an exercise in self-torture.

Huh. Self-torture is trying to do the maths on an equation you don't have all the numbers for, Nick.

"Well, that didn't go the way I thought it would."

Nick started at Jennifer's voice. Dull pain stabbed through his temple at the abrupt jerk, making him wince. He gingerly turned his gaze to his left and watched her climb the stairs to her front porch. "And what way was that?" he asked.

She gave him a wide grin, reached out and pulled his right eye open a little with confident fingers before he could move. "I kinda expected you both to be lip-locked on my bed, to be honest. That's why I stepped outside," she answered, studying his eye with a contemplative gaze. "How's your head, by the way? Splotches in your vision? Giddy? Flashing lights?"

He chuckled. "No. Does that mean my doc gives me permission to go after Lauren?"

She moved her fingers to his other eye, widening it with a gentle tug. "I've seen that expression on her face before. You go after Lauren tonight and she's going to knee-cap you."

He chuckled again, staying still as the vet who looked like an exotic princess inspected his eyeball. "Not part of my plan either."

"So what *was* your plan, Mr. Rock Star, if you don't mind me asking?" She released his eye and took a step back, her expression changing. Gone was the detached medical practitioner, and in her stead stood a woman wearing an undeniably curious air. But a wary one as well. "Until this afternoon, Lauren had said all of about ten words about you."

Nick's heart did a rapid little thud at the idea of Lauren talking about him. "What were those ten words?"

"'I went out with Nick Blackthorne once. Stupidest thing I've ever done.'"

Dull disappointment dropped into his gut. "That's twelve words."

Jennifer cocked a dark, straight eyebrow. "So it is. Now give. Apart from kissing her in my bedroom, what were you hoping to achieve by turning up here?"

The protective tone in her voice didn't escape him. "In all honesty, until I saw her in the playground, it was just to ask her to a wedding. Now..." He let out a ragged sigh. "Now I'm not leaving Murriundah without her."

"Whoa. That's a big statement to make."

Nick shrugged. "What can I say? I aim big."

Jennifer narrowed her eyes. "And are used to getting what you want."

"And am used to getting what I want," he agreed, shoving his hands into his jeans pockets. The cold was seeping into his bones. His breath grew whiter on the night. But he didn't want to go inside. He wanted to stand here on the porch in case Lauren came back.

Oh, man, you really are the romantic, aren't you? This isn't a song, Nick. This is real life. She's gone and she's not coming back tonight. Not for you, at least.

He licked his lips, his stare fixed on the last place he'd seen Lauren's taillights. "Can I ask a question?"

"Shoot."

"Is Josh's father around?"

Jennifer snorted. "If he is, I don't know it. She's never told me who he is."

"Have you asked?"

"Quite a few times."

"What about Josh? Does he know?"

Jennifer shook her head. "Not as far as I know. It doesn't seem to worry him, but then again, he's a pretty special kid. Talented soccer player and a mean guitarist."

Nick licked at his lips again. His mouth was dry.

"Now it's my turn," Jennifer was saying, her voice level. Serious. "How long ago did you and Lauren have your...thing?"

"It started twenty odd years ago." He gave her a sideward look, his pulse pounding far too fast in his neck. "Lasted a few more after that."

"So not just a casual fling then?"

Nick's chest squeezed tight. "No, not just a casual fling." He thought of all the days and nights spent with Lauren. Laughing, loving, just enjoying being with each other even if it was doing something as menial as washing the dishes after dinner. God, he missed doing the dishes. How surreal was that? He missed talking to Lauren about her day as he wiped the suds off their freshly washed plates.

An image came to him, Lauren nursing a tiny baby, her face softened with a sleepy smile, her gaze moving from the babe to Nick and back to her child. His chest squeezed again, a gripping vice that was borderline painful. "I always knew she'd make a good mother."

"She is. Very good. Not always easy with a teenage boy, mind you. Especially one as full of life as Josh."

The image of the baby in Lauren's arms became a boy—one with dark hair and blue eyes. Nick slid his gaze to Jennifer again. "How old is he?"

"Fifteen."

His breath caught in his throat at the answer Lauren wouldn't give him. Fifteen. Jesus, her son was fifteen.

Fifteen.

Jennifer was saying something. Something about Josh just having his birthday only three months ago. Something about Lauren buying him a...a...

Three months. That means the baby was born seven months after you left her. Which means she was two months pregnant and you didn't even...

"Know it," Nick murmured, a numb weight pressing down on him. All over him.

"Sorry?" Jennifer stopped, giving him a confused look. "What did you say?"

Nick shook his head, his mind whirling. "Nothing."

Her eyes narrowed. "When you say your...thing...with Lauren lasted a few years more, how many more are we talking about exactly?"

Nick ran his hand over his mouth, that pressure bearing down on him some more. Suffocating him. "It ended fifteen years ago," he said, the words like dust in his mouth. "Fifteen years and seven months to be precise."

Jennifer stared at him. "Oh, fuck."

Nick's gut clenched. His blood roared in his ears. His heart slammed into his throat. Hard. Fast.

Jesus, he had a son. He had a son to the only woman he'd ever loved and she hadn't told him.

The world swam. Sickening waves of cold pressure crashed over him. He thought of the shit of the last two years of his life. Of discovering he was adopted when his parents were killed in a car accident. Of tracking down his biological mother to a gravestone in Germany. Of learning he had a kid brother who never knew he existed either. A brother who'd been abused by his biological mother's boyfriend. A brother who'd committed suicide only months after Nick found him.

He thought of all the secrets in his life he'd never known and now this. Now he'd discovered he had a son.

A son. And he'd never known that either. Fifteen years he could have spent getting to know him. Hell, at the very least lived with the knowledge the woman he loved had borne him a child. But, as with the rest of his existence that had nothing to do with music, it was a fake reality. His family, his life, a farce. Nothing but words to a fucked-up song written by some other composer.

His whole fucking life was a lie. And Lauren, the one person he trusted, the only person he loved, had kept the most important thing a man could ever know from him.

Someone reached into his chest and ripped out his heart. Someone else slammed a fist into his gut. He stood motionless, his brain incapable of comprehending any of it. Christ, he'd come to ask her to a wedding, to say sorry for treating her like he had and now he had a son?

His knees gave out. Just like that he was stumbling sideways.

"Hey!" Jennifer's hands grabbed at his arm and hauled him back upright. "I think you need to—"

He shrugged her off, shaking his head as he did so. "I'm fine."

"Err, yeah, that's why you almost collapsed."

He shook his head again. "I'm okay."

Bullshit you are. Fuck, you've got a son. A son you never knew existed.

Why hadn't she told him?

Why hadn't Lauren told him?

You still don't know if Josh is yours. You were hardly home the last few months before you up and left her for good. She may have found someone else. You don't know—

But he did. This was Lauren. Infidelity and Lauren didn't go together.

And Nick Blackthorne and Dad do?

"I guess I should have worked it out before," Jennifer said, the words like smoke tickling at Nick's fraying nerves. "Josh looks like you. Hell, he even sounds like you, especially when he sings."

Nick's heart smashed harder, trying to splinter his breastbone. "Sings?"

Jennifer gave him an unreadable look. "I've been at

Lauren's house when Josh is playing SingStar with his best friend."

A shiver rippled over Nick's skin, making his hair stand on end. He closed his eyes, trying to picture a fifteen-year-old him. He couldn't. It was too long ago, a life too far in the past. Hell, at fifteen all he could think about was Lauren Robbins and what colour undies she was wearing. It would take a couple of years before he found out. At fifteen he'd had no clue where he'd be standing at the ripe old age of thirty-six. At fifteen, he'd had no clue he'd be who he was now.

Who's that? A rock star? Or a selfish prick?

"So, Mr. Blackthorne?" Jennifer still studied him with that guarded, ambiguous expression. Like she was half way to thinking he was about to go crazy and climb the nearest clock tower. "Do I take you to your car now? Are you driving back to Sydney? Or are you staying in Murriundah tonight?"

He blinked, the questions kicking him out of his stupor. "Do you mean am I going to do a runner now I know about my son?" He shook his head, awakening fresh pain in his temple. "No."

"But you're not going around to Lauren's tonight, are you?"

That protective edge was back in the vet's voice—a hard strength he couldn't miss even in his shell-shocked state. He gave her a small smile. "Something tells me if I said yes right now I'd find myself waking up on your sofa with a headache."

"I have the Detomidine ready to go."

Struggling to cling on to his sanity, Nick raised an eyebrow. If he focused on something else, something believable, maybe his world could make sense again. And at the moment, whatever the vet beside him was talking about was more real than the notion of him having a son. "Detomidine?"

She nodded. "Perfect for sedating big dumb animals. Will

knock out a horse in a few minutes."

He laughed, a short hollow chuckle. "Jesus, remind me never to piss you off."

"Don't hurt my best friend and we're good."

His throat filled with a heavy lump. Hurt Lauren? It seemed he'd hurt her enough to last a lifetime already. Enough for her to not tell him he had a son. Christ, how much did she have to hate him to keep something like that a secret?

And how much had *she* hurt him *now*? How did he even begin to process what he'd just discovered? Fuck, he felt like he'd been torn apart and—

"Are you staying at the Cricketer's Arms?"

He turned to Jennifer. His head ached. A lot. Christ, it felt like it was about to split open. "Their penthouse room."

She laughed, the sound nervous. The top-floor room at Murriundah's only hotel, two stories off the ground and adjacent to the communal loo, was hardly *penthouse* status. The Cricketer's Arms was, however, the only option an out-of-towner had, and that's what he was now, an out of towner. He'd stopped being a local sixteen and a half years ago.

"I tell you what," Jennifer said. "You can crash on my sofa until you figure out what you're doing next. That way I can keep an eye on your head."

"No."

She raised her eyebrows at his short answer.

His stomach lurched. He didn't need to be near anyone at the moment. He couldn't. He needed to be alone. He wanted to climb into a bottle and stay there. Drink his shock away until the hurt in his soul was drowned. Get so drunk he didn't have to consider that every time he got back on his feet he found or lost another person in his family.

He swung away from Jennifer, studying the darkness beyond her front porch. Murriundah sat silent around him, as if it felt his disbelief. "Where's my car?"

She stiffened. "Where are you going?"

"To the pub."

"To the Arms? Not to Lauren?"

He bit back a harsh growl. "No, not to Lauren." Not right at this moment. He didn't think that was smart. He wanted to ask her why she hadn't told him. He wanted to ask her if it was true, if Josh really was his son? His son.

His gut knotted.

He needed to go. Now.

He needed a drink. He needed...

Lauren.

"I've gotta go," he muttered, stepping down Jennifer's front steps. "I'll come collect my car keys tomorrow."

"I don't think—" Jennifer began, but he ignored her. He hurried away, the night's chill biting at his skin. His jacket was inside, along with the keys to his rental car, but he didn't want to go back into Jennifer's house. Not when one look at the bed's crumpled duvet would remind him immediately of what he and Lauren had been doing on it moments before she revealed she had a son. He had his wallet and his phone. That's all he needed tonight. That and a bottomless bottle of scotch.

The loose gravel on the side of the road crunched under his feet as he made his way to the Cricketer's Arms. He didn't have to orientate himself to know where to go. A person could walk from one side of Murriundah to the other in thirty minutes flat. All he needed to do was find the main drag, a straight strip of crumbling bitumen that sliced the town in two, and follow it toward the mountains overlooking the eastern end of town. He refused to think about the situation. He refused. He focused on

75

the sound his feet made, focused on putting one foot in front of the other. He wouldn't let himself think about it. Not now. Not yet.

Not until he'd had a drink.

Not until he was well and truly drunk and numb. Not until he could think about what Lauren had done without wanting to... Christ, without wanting to what? Wring her bloody neck for keeping the truth from him? Scream at her until he lost his voice—and wouldn't Walter Winchester just love that? Shake her? Hug her?

Kiss her for giving him family when he thought he had none?

Fall to his knees and sob at her feet?

Turn away from her? Run away from her—and your son?

Less than twenty minutes later he was sitting in a booth in the back of the pub, wrapped in the warmth of the Cricketer's Arms' blazing open fire, the smell of beer, old cigarette smoke and peanuts flowing through him with each breath he took. His fingertips still stung from the cold and his head still hurt—more so from the surge of blood flowing through the bruise on his temple thanks to his walk. His belly burned from the two scotches that he'd downed straight up within a minute of walking into the bar. All these sensory inputs and all he could think about was one woman and one teenage boy he'd never met.

He stared at the glass in his hand, the surface of the amber liquid within somehow glinting under the muted lights. He sat in the shadows, knowing the barkeeper was watching him. Knowing the man was about ten seconds away from recognising him. Knowing but not caring.

He lifted the glass to his lips and threw back his head, swallowing the scotch in one mouthful. It turned to liquid fire on the way to his gullet, a stream of heat that should have made him feel less numb. It didn't.

He poured another shot from the bottle he'd bought, the only bottle of Chivas Regal the Cricketer's Arms had on the shelf, and sent it down his throat after the third.

And still, he felt...

"Thirsty," he muttered, refusing to ponder how he felt. He wasn't ready.

Chicken.

Another drink burned its way to his gut, smooth fire streaming down through his being. And another.

The barkeeper watched him, the white towel hung over the man's shoulder like a white slash of purity in the muted bar. Nick poured another drink. He wondered what Lauren was doing, pictured her at her home. She turned and looked at him, giving him a smile as she passed him the popcorn. Loud noise blasted from the television, Linkin Park wailing about a divide. A massive robot ran across the screen and turned into a semi trailer, the action making the boy sitting beside Nick laugh.

His son.

Nick killed the image and poured another drink.

"Are you Nick Blackthorne?"

The question jerked his attention from the glass and he gazed at an elderly couple—maybe in their seventies—standing beside his booth. The woman had her hand resting in the crook of the man's elbow, a warm smile on her face as she waited for Nick to answer.

"I am," he said, the whiskey in his throat turning the words to a husky murmur.

The woman gave her partner a triumphant look, slapping his shoulder with a gentle smack. "See? I told you so." She turned back to Nick. "We're the Missens. You used to mow our lawn for us when you were twelve. Saving up for a guitar, I think you were."

Nick raised his eyebrows, staring at the two elderly people. They didn't seem to want to stand still. Or maybe it was the world that didn't. Or him. He licked his lips.

"What are you doing now, Nick?" the older man was asking. "Still playing the guitar?"

Nick licked his lips again, his throat hot. The side of his head hurt, a dull pain not even close to the ache in his chest. "I don't know," he answered. The words felt wrong in his mouth. Like a lie. He did know. Didn't he?

Jesus, he didn't. He didn't have a fucking clue.

He held up the glass and, eyes closed, threw its contents down his throat. And still the liquid didn't abate the chill in his soul. A quiet *tsk tsk* sounded to his left, a shuffle of feet and a whispered, "What a shame, he had such promise". He opened his eyes to find himself alone again with his bottle and ever-watchful barkeep.

There was no elderly couple

There was no Lauren either. No Lauren and no teenage son.

No one to talk to.

Fuck, he'd never felt so alone. Alone and empty and missing something. Missing her. Missing fifteen years of...of...what? Something he didn't know could have been? Missing a family he didn't know he had? Christ, what was he thinking? He was Nick Blackthorne. He didn't have time for a kid. He didn't have time for a little wife and a picket fence. He was a rock star. *The* rock star, damn it. Why the fuck was he sitting here in a pissy little pub getting drunk over a woman who hadn't told him what he'd deserved to know? Why was he even back in town? If she'd wanted him, Lauren would have come to him. Women chased him. Not the other way round. Women threw themselves at him. Wanted him. That was the way his life was. Not being a dad. Not playing soccer in the backyard, or taking his son fishing, or teaching him how to play the guitar. Not watching him take his first girlfriend out on their first date. Not helping him get over his first heartbreak. Not...not...

Not being Nick Blackthorne, rock star. M.I.A. father.

He poured another drink, the bottle chinking on the glass's edge. Whiskey splashed over the side. Not a lot, but enough to make the barkeep narrow his eyes.

Nick ignored him, turning his glass a full circle on the table. Damn it, he ached. He wanted nothing more than to look into Lauren's eyes and see his heart there, see her love. He loved her. Jesus Christ, he loved her. And it had nothing to do with how fucking amazing she looked, how fucking hot she was, how incredible she was to make love to. It had everything to do with how she made him a better person.

Clichéd, Nick. Are you really stooping to clichés?

He was. He was drunk. He was allowed to stoop to clichés. Clichés spoke the language a singer knew all too well. How many songs had he written about love? About love lost? Love denied? About futures destroyed and hope shattered.

He didn't want to be a walking cliché. He didn't. He wanted to be—

His phone vibrated in his pocket, a second before The Wiggles started singing "Hot Potato".

The barkeeper chuckled, sliding his white towel off his shoulder as he turned to the glasses stacked behind him, seemingly done with his Nick Blackthorne vigil. Nick squirmed about on the bench seat, digging his phone out of his pocket before blinking at the image on the screen. He hit the accept key, raising the phone to his ear. "Hey, Uncle As."

"Where are you, Nick?" His bodyguard's voice slid through the connection into Nick's brain, rumbly deep as always.

Nick dropped his head into his free hand. "In the Cricketer's Arms, drunk as a fart and pissed as a skunk."

"Interesting," Aslin answered. "Do I need to fire up the chopper and get there right away?"

Nick snorted. "Guess what, As?"

"What?"

Nick stared hard at his whiskey. "I'm going to be a dad."

"What?" Aslin's voice didn't slide through the connection. It punched through it.

Nick frowned, turning his glass around once on the table. "No, wait. That's wrong. I've been a father for fifteen years. I only just found out today."

"Bloody hell, Nick. Do I need to call your lawyer? Are we talking paternity suit here?"

Nick shook his head, closing his eyes on the blurry, unfocussed glass before him. "We're talking Lauren Robbins here, As."

Aslin didn't answer.

"Lauren Robbins," Nick went on, his chest suddenly tight, his stomach suddenly knotted. His balls suddenly swollen. "The woman I came back to say sorry to, has a son. My son. Isn't that a kicker?"

"Tell me what you think you're doing, Nick?"

"I don't know." He snorted. "Getting drunker?"

"I'll be there in an hour. Don't move." Aslin's accent grew thicker, his voice deeper. "And don't have anything else to drink."

The line disconnected. Nick listened to the engaged signal for a second, tapping his foot to its monotonous beat before tossing his phone onto the table. He picked up his whiskey, studied it and then drained the glass.

He'd lied to Aslin. He'd lied to the old couple, Mr. and Mrs. Missen whose lawn he'd mowed all the way through his twelfth summer. He *did* know what he was going to do now. He did.

His chest squeezed tighter. His balls throbbed.

He picked up the whiskey bottle and poured another shot.

He knew *exactly* what he was going to do now.

Whether Lauren wanted to let him or not.

He was Nick Blackthorne, after all. He always got what he wanted.

Chapter Six

Someone was banging on the front door. Continuously. Lauren rolled onto her stomach and smothered her head with her pillow. "Go away," she mumbled. Damn it, she'd only fallen asleep an hour or so ago. Finally fallen asleep after hours staring at her bedroom's dark ceiling, the sound of Nick singing "Night Whispers" emanating from her iPod beside her bed.

"And I want to beg but I can't find the words." A much younger Nick had sung to her through the night, his voice husky, the evocative sound of an acoustic guitar his only accompaniment.

"And I want to cry, but I can't find the tears.

"And all that's left is the shadow of your heart and the ghost of your smile...

"And the whispers in the night."

It had been stupid, self-torture, listening to that song over and over again. The first song he'd released after their relationship had ended. Listening to him sing the words she'd always wondered may have been written for her. Self-torture she couldn't stop. Until finally, her eyes burning with stubbornly unshed tears, she'd fallen asleep with Nick singing to her in her head.

The banging on the door continued, loud enough to penetrate the duck-down stuffing of her pillow.

Someone wanted to talk to her bad.

Nick...

Her belly flip-flopped and she groaned. "Go away," she called from under her pillow. Stupid really. Her bedroom was on the other side of the house to the front door. Whoever was on the other side—Nick?—wouldn't hear her.

Which meant she had to get up and answer it, or pretend there was no one here.

Her belly twisted. She liked option number two.

No, you don't.

"*Walking paths I haven't seen,*" Nick continued to sing, "*Looking for roads I've left behind.*"

The banging grew louder. She stretched over to her iPod dock, turned up the volume and buried her head under her pillow again.

"*It doesn't mean a thing when I know you're not there. Know you've moved on. Know you don't care.*"

More banging.

"*And all that's left is the shadow of your heart and the ghost of your smile...*

"*And the whispers in the night.*"

Even more banging, this time followed by a muffled voice she could barely hear calling out something she couldn't understand.

"Oh, for the love of God." She flung her pillow aside, climbed out of bed and squinted at the bright light streaming into her room through the window. She'd been so frazzled last night she'd forgotten to pull the blinds.

See? A perfect reason to get Nick out of your life again. He makes you forget simple things.

Her pulsed thumped a little harder at the thought. Or was

it the vaguely remembered dream coming back to her—a dream where Nick was making love to her on her bed as the curtain billowed in a warm summer breeze, the sounds of screaming fans outside chanting his name...

"The ghost of your smile," he sang from her iPod. *"And the whispers in the night."*

Lauren scrubbed her hands through her hair and hurried to the door. She must look like hell. Her hair was a mess, her PJs old and worn, her makeup from the day before smudged. Well, good. Let him see her this way. Let him see the harsh reality of Lauren Robbins, mother and teacher. Bet he never woke up with a woman wearing Elmo pyjamas before. Or with her hair looking like a bird's nest. A psychotic bird's nest.

The wooden floor of the hallway was cold, sending a rush of gooseflesh over her as she approached the doorway. Her nipples pinched tight. Her breath quickened. What was she going to say to him? What did she want to say?

Go away.

I'm sorry.

Make love to me. Please?

She curled her fingers around the door handle, released the lock and pulled the door wide.

Josh's best friend, Rhys McDowell, stood on the other side, grinning at her. "Way to rock the grunge look, Miss R."

Lauren's face flooded with heat. She let out a sharp breath, her belly flip-flopping some more. "Rhys, why are you banging on my door so early in the morning?"

He grinned some more, his blue eyes positively sparkling with ill-disguised mirth. "It's not early, Miss Robbins. It's almost ten a.m.. And Josh is meant to be at soccer in—"

"I'm coming, I'm coming!" Josh barreled past Lauren, shoving one gangly arm into his soccer shirt as he all but fell

84

across the threshold, his sport bag flopping around his back, his soccer boots clattering on the wooden porch like rapid gun fire.

Rhys smirked, staggering away from Josh seconds before Josh tossed him his bag. "You two ever heard of something called an alarm clock?"

"Shut up, McDowell," Josh laughed, thrusting his other arm into his sleeve and tugging his shirt over his head. "Like you've never been late."

Rhys chuckled, tossing Josh's bag back to him. "Yeah, but I've only been late for school. Never for something important like soccer."

Both boys laughed some more, their grins wide as they ran from the door. They jumped over the porch steps with loping grace and their feet hit the damp ground with solid thuds.

"See ya, Mum," Josh threw over his shoulder, jogging after Rhys. "I'm going to Rhys's after the game, okay?"

"See ya later, Miss R," Rhys called, the mirth in his grin just as clear in his voice. "Love the PJs!"

Lauren stood in the doorway, her mouth open. She watched the two boys sprint down the driveway, soccer bags flung over their shoulders like lumpy capes, their laughter dancing on the still morning air behind them.

A soft chuckle bubbled up her throat. Did Josh even brush his hair?

Shaking her head, she closed the door. What a way to start the day. She needed coffee. A lot of coffee. Preferably fed intravenously into her system as she attempted to make sense of the last twelve hours. Thinking it was Nick at her door was a perfect example of how quickly she would unravel if she let herself. After last night, Nick was probably back in Sydney. Or Melbourne. Or wherever the hell he actually called home now.

Anywhere but here.

"Good."

Her stomach—still churning from her rude awakening—tightened and she let out a shaky sigh. Damn it, why the hell had he come back into her life? Why? She'd done quite well without him, thank you very much. And now—*bam*—back he was, messing up her head and getting in her dreams and making her question every decision she'd made since he walked out the door of their apartment in Sydney a lifetime ago, leaving her behind.

She bit back a sigh. No good. She had to stop thinking about him. Teeth. That's what she needed to do. Clean her teeth. Clean her teeth, splash some water on her face and maybe attempt to drag a brush through her hair.

The bathroom floor tiles were as cold on her bare feet as the water she splashed onto her face. She scrubbed her teeth and brushed her hair, refusing to look at the face in the mirror before her. Not until coffee. With coffee rational thought would return, and she could get her head around the situation. What to do next. With coffee she could—

A sharp thump on her door made her jump, her heart leaping into her throat.

Lauren rolled her eyes. God, she was twitchy this morning.

She left the bathroom, ready to give Josh a hard time about forgetting something as she opened the door.

And stared straight into Nick's piercing grey eyes. "Nice pyjamas."

She ground her teeth, her throat so thick she could barely swallow. He looked haunted and tormented and sleep deprived. Black stubble covered his jaw, his hair—normally a scruffy, sexy mess—now looked like her psychotic bird had been given a building permit to set up home on his head. His clothes were crumpled. Well, his T-shirt was, his jeans were far too snug to show anything but the perfection of his long lean legs and the bulging thickness of his—

She jerked her stare back up to his face, her cheeks on fire. Oh God, where was her brain? Just because he turned up on her door looking sexy and conflicted and wretched didn't mean she could go all gooey and wanton and...and...sex-obsessed. She gripped the doorknob tighter, tilted her chin and fixed him with an unwavering glare. "What do you want, Nick. And don't say me, 'cause I'm not on your playlist anymore."

"Looking for roads I've left behind," Nick's voice wafted down the hallway, *"It doesn't mean a thing when I know you're not there. Know you've moved on. Know you don't care."*

Nick raised an eyebrow. "Seems like I'm on yours however."

Lauren closed her eyes. She dropped her head, swallowing at the lump filling her throat. "Please go away, Nick," she murmured, eyes still closed, head still down. "I can't take this."

He stepped closer to her. Close enough her nerve endings tingled. Close enough she could hear his slow intake of breath. "I can't go away, Lauren," he whispered, his hand lifting to her face. He brushed the back of his fingers against her cheek, over her lips. "I can't. God help me, please don't ask me to. Not now."

With the slightest of pressure, he lifted her chin. She couldn't stop him. She didn't want to. She let him.

"Look at me, babe." His voice caressed her lips. "Look at me and tell me not to kiss you."

She opened her eyes, gazed at him through lowered lashes. Saw the torment in his face. Saw the desire in his eyes. Desire for her. Desire she knew so well. So very well.

She parted her lips. And said, "Kiss me, Nick. Please."

He did.

His mouth took full and utter possession of hers. His

87

tongue travelled her lips, her teeth, teasing her until she crushed her body to his and tangled her fingers in his hair. She lashed her tongue over his, demanding he kiss her harder, deeper. He did as she begged, his hands roaming her back as he plundered her mouth.

A moan vibrated low in her throat. Her nipples turned into painful tips of flesh. They rubbed at the soft flannel of her PJs, the friction like a drug seeping into her mind. How did he make her feel like this? How did he make her want him so much?

It didn't matter. Not now. Now, she just wanted this kiss. Just this kiss and then she'd tell him to go. To leave.

Just this kiss.

He swiped his tongue into her mouth and captured hers, driving her back a step as he did so. She went easily, her arms wrapping around his shoulders, her fingers fisted in his hair. He wouldn't let her fall. Even though her heels stumbled on the hallway runner, he wouldn't let her fall. He would kiss her until she went insane with want and pleasure, but Nick wouldn't let her fall. She knew that. Her heart knew that.

And so she gave herself over completely to the kiss. This one wild, stupid, irresponsible kiss. Gave herself to it with greedy acceptance.

Nick's mouth plundered hers, his hands leaving her back for her hips, her breasts. He yanked at her pyjama top, seeking the buttons on her shirt. A low growl tore from his throat when he couldn't find them. Swift and almost savage, he thrust one hand under the hemline of her top and dragged his palm up over her ribcage.

His fingers found her breast, its weight unrestrained by bra or singlet. A ripple of base delight coursed through her and she let out another moan, this one louder. Nick fed from the sound, feasting on her lips and tongue. He sucked her tongue into his mouth for a split second, the action both surprising and thrilling her. It was such a possessive, dominating ownership of her mouth, of her, and her pussy flooded with damp heat.

Lord, if he plunged his hand between her thighs now his fingers would come away wet.

Because you're letting him take what he rejected fifteen years ago.

The thought seared into her. She groaned, rolling her head from his. "This can't be more than..."

He didn't let her finish. His hand closed over her breast, his mouth captured hers again. His whole body was strung tight. She could feel every muscle against her like corded steel. Nick had always been lean with sinewy strength, but the energy in his body now... Oh God, she could burn in it forever and despise herself the next day.

Yet she couldn't stop him. Didn't want to. It was too raw. Primitive.

And God help her, too right. Why did this have to feel so right? Damn him.

A sob choked in her throat and she clung to him with desperate urgency. After this he would be gone. She couldn't let him stay. After this it was just her and Josh again, and that was the way it had to be. But this kiss...this man...his hands...his mouth...

Nick's fingers closed over Lauren's breast, his palm flattening it with kneading want. He growled something against her lips, an expletive, a plea? She didn't know. His hand massaged her breast as his mouth drank from her lips, and she didn't know what he'd groaned.

She tore her face away again, the smoldering tension in the pit of her belly telling her she needed to.

He stared into her face, his nostrils flaring, his eyes the

colour of angry storm clouds. "Why…" he began, and then groaned again, dropping his head to her throat as he yanked her to his body. He pinched at her nipple, dragged his thumb over its tip. She shuddered, a whimper slipping from her. And another when his lips sucked on the sensitive flesh beneath her ear.

"Nick," she gasped, "Don't…don't leave…"

"I'm not, babe," he rasped, his breath like turbulent wind against her neck, his thigh grinding to the junction of her thighs. "No fucking way."

"A mark," she panted. "Don't leave…"

He sucked harder on her throat, his fingers sinking into her breast. She bucked to him, her pussy throbbing, her nails raking at his scalp. Damn him. Why did he have this power over her? Why did he… How could he still do this to her? After so many years? After so many nights crying into her pillow? Wishing him dead. Wishing him in her arms.

As if he felt the torment cutting through her, he lifted his head and gazed down at her. Grey pain boiled in his eyes, pain and desire and want and need. The skin around his nose stretched tight. His Adam's apple jerked up and down in his throat.

"This doesn't change anything, Nick." The words were acid on her tongue. "It can't. It's just…"

"Why…" he began, voice like stripped smoke. He closed his eyes again, jaw bunching. "Fuck, Lauren, why didn't…"

Whatever he was going to ask was lost on a groan. A groan that turned into a ragged pant as he kicked the door shut behind him and crushed her lips with his, once again kissing her with such fierce hunger it frightened her.

Frightened her and aroused her to a place she'd never been.

Her sex wept, contracted on Nick's dick. Except it wasn't there. It wasn't buried in her core. It rubbed her belly, long and hard and imprisoned by his trousers. She fought to release it, her fingers snatching at his fly. She wanted his swollen length in her hand, in her mouth, in her cunt. She writhed against him, bare feet slapping on the floor as he spun around and propelled her backward.

Her arse hit the door first. His hips ground against her second. He fucked her mouth with his tongue, plundering, taking, possessing. And all the while his hands raked her body. Under her shirt, over her ribs, capturing her breast. She moaned, the sound turning to a cry when he pulled her pyjama top over her head and tossed it aside.

He captured one nipple, suckled hard, and then moved his mouth back to her lips, his hands raking over her body once more. Down her waist, over her hips, beneath her pyjama pants. He explored her arse cheeks through her undies, his fingers tugging at the skimpy cotton knickers until they were bunched under her backside. He squeezed and kneaded and caressed her flesh, his fingers pulling at her cheeks until they stroked over the puckered hole of her anus. She bucked, the contact like a shot of pure pleasure straight into her core.

Nick groaned into her mouth, yanked his mouth from hers and, with a sudden, violent move, stripped her of her pyjama pants and knickers. The cool hallway air kissed her bare skin, a heartbeat before his lips did the same. He plunged his tongue between her thighs, licking at her folds with seeking need. She shifted her legs, unable to do anything else but grant him greater access to her sex.

He took it. Sucked at her pussy lips. Laved them with his tongue. Stabbed it in and out of her heat. She whimpered, her breath hitching in her throat, her pussy flooding with eager wetness. "Want it, Nick," she mumbled, rolling her head against

91

the door, her hands in his hair. "Want it."

He parted her folds with his fingers, flicking at her clit. She hissed. Lord, it felt so good. So damn good.

"I've missed your taste, babe." He rolled a finger over her clit, fast little circles that sent wicked bolts of liquid tension into her very centre. "Missed your taste, your smell...the feel of your cream on my lips..."

He lapped at her sex again, wriggling a finger into her slit as his tongue teased her clit. She gasped, her toes curling, her knees trembling. Oh God, if he kept this up she was going to come on his face.

As if he heard her very thoughts, or knew her very want, he placed her right thigh over his shoulder, fucking her more thoroughly with his tongue. She cried out, her nails scraping at his scalp. "Nick, I-I think..."

He nipped her clit with gentle teeth and sucked it better, the action turning her words to whimpering sounds. The more he lavished her pussy with his mouth, his fingers, the more she lost herself to the pleasure. The only man who had ever tasted her was eating her out against her front door and nothing else mattered. Nothing else existed except Nick's mouth on her sex and the pleasure swelling through her.

Nothing else existed except his tongue in her—

He stood, her leg sliding from his shoulder. He pulled his shirt over his head and threw it aside, his hands going to his fly straight after. She helped him, needing his dick. Lord, she needed his dick. More than she needed air. She needed it inside her.

And then it was in her hand, long and thick and so hard it throbbed. So hard and so warm and so hers. Hers.

"Can't wait, babe," he groaned, the words panted breaths against the side of her neck. "Oh, fuck, I can't...condom...need..."

She had them. Somewhere in the house. Bought for Josh the day she found him necking with a girl at the soccer fields. Bought but never given. The girl hadn't lasted, and she'd lost her nerve. But the condoms were still here. Somewhere.

Nick closed his hand around hers, stilling her pumping motion. "I need..." he choked, lips scalding her throat, her chin. "Jesus, Lauren, I'm going to fucking come on your hand if you don't..."

Pre-come wet her fingers. His breath fanned her face before he was kissing her again. Kissing her face, her temple, her throat as he squeezed his cock with her hand. As he fucked her gripping fingers. And before she knew it the word was on her lips, lips being bitten and nibbled by his. "Pill," she burst out on a breath. "I'm on the—"

He was inside her before she could finish the sentence. Inside her, stretching her. Pumping into her, one hand yanking her leg up around his hip, squeezing her arse, the other cupping and kneading her breast, pinching her nipple.

He was inside her, filling her, and she cried out. Clung to him. Squeezed him with her inner muscles, wanting more. More. So much more. And he gave it to her, a long, deep, driving thrust that pushed her faster and faster and faster to the edge. An edge she knew. The most exquisite, consuming, rapturous edge. An edge she'd balanced on so many times before with him.

"Come for me, babe," he panted, lips on hers, "Come for me."

She did. A shuddering convulsion claimed her core. Fire singed up her spine. The soles of her feet tingled, and she came, his name tearing from her throat, his flesh buried in hers, their bodies joined. She came and then he was coming with her, his cock pumping inside her, his rhythm wild and frantic. His hands held her, gripped her. His moans became something else, something primitive and primal. The sound of utter release and absolute pleasure. The very sounds falling from her lips in shallow, moaning cries of surrender.

They climaxed together, as they had always done, from the very first time a lifetime ago, their sweat slicking each other's bodies, their juices wetting each other's thighs.

Lost to everything but the elemental connection of body and soul.

Until both were spent. Until both rode the last of their climax and strength threatened to desert them.

Lauren slumped against the door, her eyes closed. Her pulse pounded, an echo of the orgasm still fading within her. Oh God, she'd just had sex with Nick Blackthorne. Unbelievable, soul-wrenching sex. She pressed a trembling hand to her lips, a sob catching in her throat. Lord, was she truly so weak? So...so...messed up?

"I'm sorry."

His hoarse murmur against the curve of her neck opened her eyes. A chill rippled over her. "Sorry?"

"I..." He stopped, his arms holding her, his lips on her neck, his body tense. Still.

"Why are you sorry, Nick?" Her mouth went dry. The reality of the situation hit her. The cold fact. She'd just had unprotected sex with Nick Blackthorne. A man she hadn't seen in fifteen years. A man who, according to every gossip and celebrity magazine the world over, never spent a night in his bed alone. A whirlwind of disconnected words lashed through her head, words no careful, intelligent woman should ever think about. Words connected to doctors and clinics and shame.

But you weren't careful. You never were with Nick. And any intelligence you have is destroyed the second he kisses you.

She pushed at his chest, forcing him off her. He complied, but only a little, staring down at her with haunted eyes. His hands still cupped the back of her neck, his fingers still on her jaw. A numb pressure settled against her ears. Her lips tingled. "Did you just give me a..." She couldn't bring herself to say it.

Pained anger etched his face. "I would *never* give you a sexually transmitted disease, Lauren. I've been a bastard to you, I know, but I'm not a prick. I'm clean. 100%."

"So why are you sorry?"

"I should have stopped. I should have put on a condom. So there's no chance of me getting you pregnant."

Her mouth went dry. "Why do you think I'd get pregnant, Nick? I told you I was on the pill."

"You were on the pill before."

The simple response made Lauren's throat slam shut. Her stomach tried to leap up through it. Her breath choked her.

He didn't blink. Nor did he let her go. "Why didn't you tell me, Lauren? Why didn't you tell me fifteen years ago you were pregnant? Why didn't you tell me I had a son?"

Oh God. She stared at him. No words came. None. Just a deafening roar in her ears and a cold in her soul. *Oh God. He knows. He knows and you should have told him fifteen years ago.*

He studied her, brushing the fingertips on one hand over her bottom lip. "Why didn't you tell me, babe?" he whispered. "Why?"

Someone thumped on the door. A steady rapping of knuckles. The vibrations shot through Lauren like a spray of bullets. She let out a startled cry, every muscle in her body locking.

Nick's nostrils flared. He stepped backward, his hands sliding from her face, his jaw clenched. She watched him move away, wanting nothing more than to throw herself at him, wrap her arms around his waist and cling to him. Feel his heat seep into her body. Feel it melt away the chilled emptiness spreading through her. Hold him, be held by him. It was where she was meant to be.

It was the farthest place she wanted to be.

He'd hurt her. He'd rejected her. He'd left her.

And she'd hurt him back. By denying him his son.

"Nick," she began, watching him tuck himself back into his jeans.

The knock rapped on the door again. Just as quick. Just as expectant.

She turned away from him, unable to see the pain, the betrayal in his eyes anymore. Snatching up her pyjama shirt, she pulled it on and buttoned it with fingers that seemed to refuse her brain's commands. Fingers that fumbled and shook. Damn it, where were her pyjama pants?

The knock came again. "Ms. Robbins?" a male voice called from the other side.

She looked for her pants. Where the hell were her pants?

Fuck it. You don't need them. Your shirt's long enough. Just answer the door, get rid of whoever is on the other side and then tell Nick you're sorry. Tell him you still love him. Tell him you were wrong. Tell him everything.

She shot Nick a look over her shoulder. He stood a few steps behind her, half-dressed, his upper body naked and still slicked in a fine sheen of sweat, his chest rising and falling with each steadying breath he pulled, his lean muscles sculpted and defined with the exertion of their fucking. His fly was zipped, the top of the treble cleft tattooed on his lower abdomen peaking from above the low-slung waistline of his jeans. His thick black hair hung around his face, awry from her hands, brushing eyes that studied her with an unreadable intensity.

He looked like a sexual god.

He looked like a rock star.

Closing her eyes, she raked her fingers through her hair, took a deep breath and then turned back to the door and pulled it open.

White light exploded in her eyes. Soundless. Blinding. White light followed by Nick snarling, "You fucking prick, Holston."

White light speared into her eyes again. A flash so bright she gasped.

"Having a good time, Blackthorne?" the man in front of her asked, although it wasn't so much a question but a chuckling sneer. And she couldn't see him. All she could see was painful yellow glare dancing on her retina, glaring yellow light making it impossible to see, just like the kind left over from a powerful camera flash.

Camera.

She blinked. She could see a man on her front step, and yet she couldn't. He was hiding behind the dancing yellow burn from his camera's flash.

"You guys need to get a life," she heard Nick growl. And then he was pushing past her. White light exploded in front of her again as the man's voice called out, telling her to smile, to give Nick a kiss, asking her how long they'd been together. White, rapid-fire flash bombs accompanied by the distinct click of a camera attacked her, capturing her stupor seconds before the sound of her door slamming shut smacked at her ears.

She stared at Nick, her pulse not only thumping in her neck but in her temples. She stared at him through the yellow brand on her retina as Holston continued to call out from the other side of her door, asking how long she and Nick had been lovers, if she always slept in Elmo pyjamas, if—

"I'm sorry." Nick reached for her, his hands smoothing up her arms. "You didn't need to experience that. Holston's an unethical prick. I don't know how he even knew I was Murriundah."

Red anger smashed into her. Scalding hot in its clarity. It all came rushing back to her—the minutes spent with Nick in public, the screaming fans, the stalking photographers, the other women calling her names and sending her hate mail. All of it. And now here it was on her doorstep? No. She wasn't standing for it. She jerked out of his gentle hold and stepped away from him. Her hip struck the hall console table, sharp pain shooting through her like an electrical jolt, but she ignored it.

"You ask why I didn't tell you, Nick? You wonder why I don't want you back in my life? Why I don't want you in *Josh's* life?" She pointed a finger at the closed door, Holston's calls and shouts a muffled, grating noise on the other side. "*There's* your answer. Now please, get the rest of your clothes and go. Leave me alone, get out of my life and take your goddamn paparazzo with you."

He stood motionless, watching her. He didn't move. Not a muscle twitched. He didn't move and he didn't take his stare from her face.

"Leave," she ground out, hating the waver in her voice. *Hating* it, damn him. "Now."

He stayed like a statue for another painful heartbeat before letting out a ragged sigh. "It's not always like this, Lauren."

She shook her head. "Don't, Nick. I was there at the beginning, remember?"

He studied her, a long silent gaze that made her already tight chest squeeze tighter. He looked broken. Defeated. Nick Blackthorne, rock star, stripped away of all his arrogant, self-assured charm. He looked like the boy she'd first met waiting for the high school bus twenty-one years ago. The boy whose family had just moved to Murriundah from Sydney. The boy called a fag because he didn't want to be on the school rugby team. The boy picked on by the older kids, the jocks, for taking a guitar to and from school. The boy whose voice was breaking, whose face was marked by acne and who would only a few years later be discovered one summer Sunday afternoon playing that same guitar in the Cricketer's Arms by a US talent agent on a working vacation in the backwater towns of Australia. A US talent agent looking for the next big thing.

The next big thing who would take the world by storm and destroy her heart in the process.

"Please leave, Nick," she asked again, the request no more than a whisper. "I won't let your life destroy Josh's."

Wordlessly, he reached behind him and withdrew a phone from his back pocket. He slid his thumb over the screen a few times before lifting it to his ear without taking his gaze from her face. "Come get me, Aslin," he said, voice steady. Composed.

Cold emptiness welled in Lauren's stomach. She fought the need to close her eyes, to bite her lip and hug herself. Instead, she watched him gather up his shirt and pull it over his head. She watched him dress, unable to say a word, refusing to listen to the words she *wanted* to say—*stay, I'm sorry, love me.* She couldn't listen to them. This was the way it had to be, no matter how irrevocably he owned her body, her soul. This is the way it had to be for her sanity.

How it had to be for her son's wellbeing.

Are you sure you're thinking of Josh here? Are you?

"Fuck off, Rhodes," Holston suddenly shouted, his voice much more distant than before, and Lauren started, realising she hadn't heard him for the duration of Nick's dressing. She hadn't heard anything but the thump thump of her stupid heart and the soft *shhh* of material sliding over skin. Nick's skin.

She blinked, jerking her stare to the closed door. The paparazzo shouted something again, something that sounded like, "Go back to England, you Pommie bastard," and someone else laughed, a short sharp chuckle filled with mirth followed by a sharp double knock on her door.

Nick let out a sigh. "That's my bodyguard."

When she didn't say anything, he opened his mouth, closed it again, dragged his fingers through his hair and then turned to the door and opened it.

A massive man dressed in black jeans, black T-shirt and black leather jacket stepped across the threshold, his shoulders so broad he almost had to turn sideways to pass through the doorway. His direct blue gaze slid over everything with intense scrutiny, marking everything, missing nothing, before settling on Lauren. He studied her, took in her bare legs, her hastily buttoned pyjama shirt, her disheveled hair. If he thought anything of her state, he didn't show it. "Ms. Robbins," he said, a subtle British accent rolling through her name.

She stared back at him, his sheer presence turning her pulse to a rapid trip hammer. She'd seen images of the man in magazines and on the television, always shadowing Nick or clearing a path through a squealing, writhing crowd, but no photograph conveyed the absolute size of him. The latent menace that oozed from him in waves. The intimidating, controlled power.

Lord, he looked like he could snap a person in two with barely an effort.

Of course he could, Lauren. He's Nick's bodyguard. He's got to be able to hold back every screaming fan, maniacal groupie or whacked-out psycho who thinks Nick is his best friend.

The thought made her scowl. As did the overwhelming worry for Nick's safety that came with it. She didn't want to be worried for Nick. She'd been there, done that and burnt the T-shirt. She wasn't going to do it again.

She couldn't.

"This is not how I planned anything, Lauren."

She turned to Nick, her chest so tight she wondered if she would ever draw breath again. She looked at him, trying to see the rock star, seeing only the man she fell in love with oh so many years ago.

The man she could never let go. The man she would worry about until time ceased.

She wanted to tell him to stay. Wanted, but wouldn't.

"All I wanted was to share a moment of reality with you," he said. "A day of being just a guy taking the girl of his dreams somewhere wonderful and joyous."

She caught her bottom lip with her teeth.

"We need to go, Nick," Aslin's voice rumbled, "preferably before Holston retrieves his camera from where I pegged it and comes back."

Nick nodded once, never taking his gaze from hers. "There's still more to say, Lauren," he said. "More to say and more to hear."

He turned away from her then. Half a second before the door flung open and Josh came charging through it.

"Mum!" he shouted. "There's a helicopter parked on the—" He ran slap-bam in Aslin.

"What the fuck?" he yelped, staggering backward.

"Josh!" Lauren snapped. God, what was he doing home? Now?

But it didn't matter. It didn't matter because her son was staring open-mouthed at Nick. Open-mouthed and wide-eyed and rooted to the spot. He swung his head, only his head, and gaped at her, and she bit back a groan of dismay at the excited disbelief on his face, a face so like his father it made her stomach knot.

"Mum?" he croaked. "Why is Nick Blackthorne standing in our house?"

Chapter Seven

Nick stared at the tall, lanky boy standing but a few feet away from him. No, he didn't just stare at him, he devoured him. His son. Jesus, he was looking at his son. Sound ceased to exist. The world became nothing but one boy, one teenage kid with scruffy black hair, freckles and wide grey eyes wearing a dirt-smeared soccer uniform and a shell-shocked expression. One boy staring back at him.

He sucked in a breath, unable to blink. He was numb. No, he was thrumming with so much energy he was going to burn up. No, he was...he was... Jesus, he was looking at his son.

His son who had no idea who he was.

The thought punched Nick in the gut. Hard. And the world rushed back at him.

"Mum?" Josh was saying. "Why is Nick Blackthorne standing in our house?" Nick listened to every vowel and consonant and syllable, noting the timbre and rhythm in his son's speech. Josh's voice must have only recently broken. It was deep, with just the slightest hint of a crack on the odd note. But there was a music to it as well, a strength. It rolled over Nick like a warm wave, making his gut clench and his chest squeeze.

"Mum?" Josh repeated, and Nick started, jerking his attention to Lauren.

She stood as still as he did, her lips parted, her stare jumping between him and her son—*their* son—her cheeks growing pale even as a warm flush painted her throat.

She didn't say a word.

Tell him. Tell him now. Fuck a duck, Nick, every family member you've ever had has been ripped from your life, taken from you, and now here's your son, standing right here, asking why you're here. Tell him. Tell him who you are.

His heart smashed faster. He licked his lips, sensing Aslin move behind him. But it was only a distant recognition. His focus was on his son. And the woman he'd stupidly left behind way too many years ago.

Tell him.

Josh gaped at his mother, at him, back to his mother again. "Is anyone going to say somethin'?"

Nick looked at Lauren. Saw the conflict tearing at her. Saw it swimming in her eyes. Saw it. Felt it.

He stepped forward, extending his hand as he did. "Hi, Josh." He wrapped his fingers around his son's hand, giving it a firm shake. A fissure of something elemental, something beyond his ability to understand shot through him at the palm-to-palm contact with the teenager, and he hid his intake of breath on a low chuckle. "Your mum and I knew each other a long time ago. I just thought I'd pop in and say hello."

He heard Lauren make a little noise and flicked her another quick look. She was watching him, her face an ambiguous mask, her body tense. But on her lips was a smile, a small smile that filled him with such an overwhelming urge to take her hand and pull her into his embrace that for a surreal moment he almost reached for her.

"You did?" Josh turned to Lauren, staring at her with open awe, and Nick's chest squeezed. "That's epic."

Nick laughed, dropping Josh's hand. He didn't want to. He didn't know what he wanted to do, but breaking contact wasn't it. What if he never got the chance again? What if his son was ripped away from him before he even got the chance to hold him?

"I've downloaded all your albums," Josh said, his face alight. Nick could almost see the excitement sparking through him. "Legally, of course. And I just started teaching myself how to play 'Gotta Run' on my guitar. It's a hard fucker to get the chords—"

"Josh," Lauren's voice drew out the boy's name, turning it to a firm warning.

Josh ducked his head, cheeks turning redder. "Sorry, Mum." He grinned at Nick from under the shaggy strands of his thick dark hair. Hair that drove the girls crazy with distraction, Nick suspected. "I mean, it's a hard song to get right."

Nick chuckled. "You're telling me. In fact, I think I said something very similar to your mum when I was writing it."

Josh gaped at Lauren, and Nick couldn't help but smile as her cheeks filled with a faint pink tinge. He'd written the entire song, his very first Australian number one, in bed with her one lazy summer weekend. Neither of them had been dressed. Her lips had travelled his chest, his stomach, his cock as he'd scrawled the words and notes down on loose sheets of paper. His temperature had risen with each caress, his heart thumping as she played his body like an instrument. She'd brought him to the brink of orgasm over and over again, teasing him with fulfillment when he finished each chorus, only giving it to him when the song was done and his cock so hard, so fucking hard he shot his load the second she slid down his length. He shifted his feet at the memory of that weekend, his groin tightening. And by the look of Lauren's flushed face, the way her breath grew quicker, she remembered it too.

Oh, Nick, you had it all. Why the fuck did you let it go?

"Is that your helicopter near the soccer fields?" Josh asked, and Nick blinked, yanked back to the here and now. "Freaked us all out when we saw it. Rhys reckoned it must belong to some drug lord camped up in the mountains."

"Really, Josh?" Lauren rolled her eyes, shaking her head, her cheeks still flushed with a heat Nick wanted to feel with his lips. Christ, he wanted that. That and so much more. "Drug lords? That's your reason for a helicopter turning up here? I think I'm cancelling our satellite TV subscription."

"*I* didn't think that. Rhys did. I said it probably belonged to the dude Mr. McGimmons had been selling his *race-horse* stock to. Said the dude finally realized the race horses couldn't run for—"

"Josh!"

Nick laughed again, giving Lauren a grin. He couldn't help it. The whole situation made him feel...feel...fuck, it made him feel alive. "It *is* mine," he answered. "Well, I assume it is." He turned and gave the silent hovering Aslin behind him a questioning look. "You didn't just steal someone's chopper, did you, As? It is mine, yes?"

Aslin's expression—calm but at the same time serious—didn't change. "It's actually Wolfmother's. Yours wasn't filled up."

Josh laughed. As did Lauren. A genuine laugh, relaxed and soft and so perfect, so musical Nick's stomach clenched. And it hit him. He wanted this. Being a family. Being a part of something more than just a life of empty hotel rooms and soulless award shows and superficial people at superficial parties. He wanted *this*. Her. Josh. Laughter. Love.

Life. Real life.

The life fate had offered him the day he met Lauren.

He wanted it. All of it.

"Okay, hot shot." Lauren's humor-laced voice stroked at his senses and he blinked, his throat tightening when he realized she wasn't agreeing to his unspoken desire but talking to Josh instead. "Time to go wash up for lunch."

Nick felt his pulse quicken. She was going to tell him to leave now. He could see it in the way she looked at him. The smile for her son still played with her lips, but her eyes were guarded once more. Guarded. Unreadable. She was going to tell him to leave and he didn't want to. Not at all.

Josh gave Nick a wide grin. "Are you staying?"

I'm not going anywhere, Josh.

The answer formed in Nick's mind. At the very moment a solid thud sounded on Lauren's front porch, followed by a muttered curse.

Aslin ground out a muttered word that may have been fuck. He flicked Nick a dark scowl. "Holston."

Nick cocked an eyebrow.

With a slow smile, Aslin turned to Lauren. "If it's okay, can I ask you to put up with the rock star here for a while longer? Just while I deal with the moron outside? I'd rather get Holston out of the road before Nick walks back to the Cricketer's Arms."

For the first time in his life, Nick sent out a silent thank you to a member of the paparazzi. *Perfect timing, Holston. Remind me to send you a Ferrari.*

"Fuck, yeah," Josh burst out. And then stared at his mother, eyes wide. "Shit. Sorry, Mum."

Lauren gazed at them both, her expression as ambivalent as her eyes. She pulled a slow breath, the action making her breasts rise, pushing them against the soft material of her pyjama shirt. Nick felt his groin stir, but he shut down the response, putting the memory of those perfect, lush breasts from his mind. Just.

Aslin raised his eyebrows. "Ms. Robbins?"

"Okay. As long as the rock star is fine with toasted-cheese sandwiches."

Nick couldn't stop his smile. "The rock star is." And Lauren knew that. They'd been his favourite winter indulgence from as far back as he could remember, his specialty whenever he *cooked* for them both, and the only meal he'd requested on his birthdays.

"Excellent." Josh's grin split his face. "Can I call Rhys, Mum? Ask him to come 'round?"

Much to Nick's amusement, Lauren lifted an eyebrow at their son—their son, Christ he loved the sound of that. "Do you really want to share Nick with Rhys, Josh?"

Josh studied her, snapped his gaze to Nick, narrowed his eyes, eyes the very grey as Nick's own, and then swung back to Lauren again. "Next time."

Nick burst out laughing.

"I'll be back in a while, Nick." Aslin put a hand on his shoulder, fixing him with a steady, pointed look. A look that told him not to waste his time.

With a nod at Lauren and a wide grin at Josh, the man pulled open the door and crossed the threshold in one giant step. Nick heard Holston's muttered curse followed by feet scrambling on the wooden porch, and then Aslin closed the door behind him, leaving Nick alone with the two people who meant more to him than he could ever express. Now if only he could be given the chance to do so.

He swallowed, suddenly completely unsure what to do next. His stare found its way to Lauren's face, to her soft lips, her clear blue eyes. For the first time he noticed fine lines at their edges, lines that told him of a life lived without him. They looked beautiful on her. Beautiful and secretive and compelling. Once again, he was overwhelmed with the need to place his lips to her face, to trace those tiny lines with his kisses. To explore her beauty with his lips as he smoothed his hands around her waist and pulled her to his body, as he held her close and rediscovered everything about her he'd never forgotten.

"Mum?"

He started at Josh's voice, his heart racing when he saw Lauren do the same thing. She blinked, licking her lips, her hands flittering to her face as she dragged her stare from Nick's.

"What's up, Josh?" There was a tremble to the words, a strained need Nick felt all the way to his core. As much as she tried to deny it, and she did, he could see it in every nuance in her body, every ragged breath she took. She was as affected by him as he was her.

Affected? Huh, don't you mean undone? Undone and remade and turned inside out?

"Why are you wearing only your pyjama shirt?"

Her cheeks turned scarlet. "Err..."

Nick choked back a laugh before it could escape him. Thankfully, Josh didn't seem interested in the answer. "Can you sign something for me?" he asked Nick instead. "I've got your first album on CD in my room. Every time I play it Mum tells me to either turn it off or put my headphones on." He slid Lauren a quick sideward glance. "I don't think she likes it much."

"That's it, Josh," Lauren crossed the small space between them in two steps and snared him in a head lock, a hilarious move considering he was almost as tall as Nick. "You're in sin-bin. Go. Now. And don't come back out until you're clean and ready to be nice to your mother."

Josh laughed, squirming out of her grip and shoving her

away with a gentle push. "Yeah, yeah. I'm going to have a shower. Try not to be too embarrassing in front of Nick while I'm gone." He turned his grin on Nick, and for a split second it was like looking in a mirror from fifteen years ago. The eyes, the hair, the face not yet a man's but not really a kid any more. Even if Nick hadn't known who Josh's father was, that grin, that cheekiness, would have screamed it loud and clear. It was enough to make his head spin. And his chest heavy with a powerful, indescribable pride.

He was a father.

"You'll still be here when I get out?" Josh asked. An anxious tension fell over the boy and Nick could see, as desperately as he was trying to play it cool, Josh was more nervous and excited then he was letting on.

A chuckle bubbled up inside Nick's heart. Like mother, like son.

He gave Josh a wide smile and said the words he knew to be truer than any he'd uttered in his life. "It's okay, mate. I'm not going anywhere."

Josh balled his fist. "Yes." He grinned at his mother again and was gone, half-running, half-loping down the hallway until he ducked into a room to his right and was gone from Nick's sight.

"You can't mess with him, Nick."

The level statement jerked Nick's attention back to Lauren. She stood still, her arms folded over her chest, her eyes worried.

"He's too great a kid to mess with. I won't let you do that to him. I know how hard it is to get over you. I won't let you do that to my son."

"*Our* son," he said. "And you just heard me. I'm not going anywhere."

She studied him, her stare moving over his face as if she

hunted answers to questions she hadn't voiced.

Ask them, Lauren. Please ask them.

"Don't do this to me again, Nick," she whispered. "Don't make me believe in something that can't happen."

He took a step toward her. "Why can't it? We're both older now. Wiser. Why can't we have what we always wanted?"

She didn't answer. Instead, she let out a sigh and turned away from him. "I'm going to make toasted cheese sandwiches," she said over her shoulder as she began walking. "You still take yours with double cheese and Vegemite?"

He swallowed, forcing a smile to his face. "You better believe it."

"Just like your son," he heard her mutter with a shake of her head. And then she laughed, a soft little chuckle, and his heart soared.

He followed her into the kitchen, taking in the tidy counter tops, the organized clutter. On the fridge was a collection of drawings, some on paper browning with age, Josh's name scrawled on the top corner, some on newer paper with other names. Those had pictures of a woman with long pink hair and a big happy smile accompanied by words like, *To Miss Robbins, love Thomas. Dear Miss, From Chloe. My best teacher, by Heidi.* Drawings of a beloved teacher by students lucky enough to spend five days a week with her. He studied those artworks, his lips curling into a smile. He was jealous of those students. Insanely jealous.

"Can you pass me a knife, please?"

He turned away from the fridge and crossed the kitchen, stopping beside Lauren at the counter. She was pulling thick slices of brown bread from a loaf, her back to him. He looked around, finding what he thought must be the utensils drawer. It was, and he wrapped his fingers around a butter knife and

111

turned to her.

Her lips met his before he could pass her the knife, her hands snaking up around the back of his neck, her fingers threading into his hair. She kissed him, her lips and tongue taking searing, slow, sensual possession of his mouth. She kissed him, and just as he slid his arms around her waist, just as his cock pulsed with eager want and he pulled her hips to his, she stopped and slipped from his hands, turning back to the waiting bread.

Nick sucked in a long breath, fighting for calm. He studied her profile, his balls swelling, his lips still wet from her kiss. "What was that?"

She didn't take her attention from the sandwich she'd started to fix. "An itch scratched."

He raised an eyebrow, his body on fire. It would be so easy to snake his arms around her and haul her against him right now. Crush her mouth with his, slip her buttons free and capture her breasts with his hands. So easy. But with Josh likely only minutes away from finishing his shower, he couldn't. He wouldn't. When he told Josh he was his dad, it was going to be face-to-face, calm and steady and certain. Not busted feeling up his mum in the kitchen.

Later maybe, months perhaps, being busted by Josh feeling up his mum wouldn't be so much a problem, would be par for the course in a family home populated by a couple blissfully in love, but at the moment...no, not the way to break the news to him.

So he placed the knife on the counter beside the loaf of bread and jar of Vegemite and retrieved the cheese from the fridge. He wouldn't let himself consider the possibility of such a euphoric, utopian happy-ever-after not eventuating. He would *make* it happen. How could Lauren kiss him like that if she didn't feel for him what he felt for her? What she'd felt for him so many years ago?

She couldn't. He just had to show her that.

By making this lunch together perfect.

Five silent-stretching minutes later, Josh came bounding into the kitchen, hair dripping, gangly limbs hidden by baggy jeans and an AC/DC T-shirt. He carried a CD and black Sharpie, and Nick noticed the nervous energy radiating from him again. "Are you sure you're okay with signing it?" He handed the CD case to Nick, a shy smile at the edges of his mouth. "I'm not going to sell it on Ebay or anything. I promise."

Nick laughed. "Oh, well, in that case." He placed the case on the counter and looked at its cover artwork. He stared at himself, sixteen years younger than he was now, his face a pouty mask of smoldering torment and contempt. His first album.

Pulling the marker's lid off with his teeth, he stared at the case, pen poised in his hand.

"Josh, can you grab Nick a drink, please?" Lauren's voice played over Nick's senses. "There's apple cider in the fridge in the garage and lemons in the fruit bowl."

A soft beat fluttered at Nick's temple and a smile spread his lips. She remembered his favourite drink—cider and lemon— and was making his favourite lunch.

He looked at the CD case lying on the counter before him, bent slightly at the waist and wrote, *Josh. Play it loud and play it often. I'll deal with your mum when you do. Promise.* He paused for a second, and then signed *Nick.*

The smell of melting cheese and toasting bread seeped into the long breath he pulled, and with it came an onslaught of memories and images and sensory ghosts. How many toasted cheese sandwiches had Lauren made for him in their life

113

together? Too many to count. How many had he had in the last fifteen years? None.

"Heads up, Nick," Lauren said, and he turned and saw her place two fully stacked plates on the table. She graced him with a quick smile, the thick curtain of her hair—still tousled from sleep and his hands and their earlier lovemaking—tumbling over her shoulder. The desire to feel those cool silken strands sliding against his skin once more was a palpable taunt. To use her very phrase—an itch that needed scratching. And so he did. He crossed to her in three quick steps and combed her hair away from her temple with a single gentle stroke of his fingers.

Her eyes fluttered closed. She turned her face to his hand and pressed her mouth to his palm.

"Drinks," Josh called out, and Nick jumped. But not as violently as Lauren. She jerked away from him, spinning back to the counter to retrieve the last plate of toasted sandwiches just as Josh loped into the kitchen, two bottles of apple cider in one hand and a lemon in the other.

He deposited them on the counter beside his mum and then hurried over to where Nick had left the CD.

"Dude." His laughter bounced around the small room. "I am so going to hold you to that."

"What?" Lauren frowned at him, flicking Nick a sideward glance.

Josh grinned at her, holding up his signed CD case. "He promised to deal with you every time I play this album." He laughed again, his grin widening as he turned to Nick. "Which means you're pretty much going to have to move in, Nick, cause I plan on playing it every day."

Nick dropped into a chair and reached for the sandwich sitting on the plate in front of him. "You know what, Josh?" He bit into the grilled cheese, the warm gooey cheddar, salty

Vegemite and toasted bread the second most delicious thing he'd tasted all day. "I'm completely down with that plan."

Josh dropped into the chair beside him and scooped up his own toasted delicacy from its plate. "You see, Mum? I *told* you you'd find a boyfriend this year. Who woulda thought it'd be Nick Blackthorne?"

Nick choked on a mouthful of toasted bread and cheese. Lauren sat in the chair opposite, her face calm and completely unreadable. She gave Nick a crocked smile, one eyebrow cocking as she lifted her sandwich to her lips. "Lucky me," she said, and took a bite.

Chapter Eight

Lunch was wonderful. Damn it.

Nick was funny, relaxed, casual, self-effacing and charming. He regaled them both with tales of his life, painting lavish details about tantrums thrown by *other* recording artists. Recording artists that, according to Nick had "to remain nameless for fear they will hunt me down and slice my...ahems...off". He told them wild stories about tour mishaps, about some of the more bizarre fan mail he'd received. He spoke about the nervous anticipation he would endure every time he was up for an award. He had them both in stitches as he showed them his practice routine for the perfect oh-crap, I-didn't-win-it-but-I-have-to-still-look-happy face. He sang them a rather twisted version of "Gotta Run" he'd learnt while touring India, his Indian accent atrocious, his smile infectious.

He talked about growing up in Murriundah with the only cop in town for a father and then told them highly exaggerated stories of Lauren's supposed adventures when they were school together, even informing Josh in a loud whisper about the time she was put on detention for kissing a boy behind the sports equipment shed. He left out that the said boy was him.

That Lauren's heartbeat tripled at the memory of that kiss—their first—made her want to smack him. But she couldn't. Not when he made her laugh so much. Not when her face ached from smiling, damn him. He entertained them both, and answered every question Josh threw at him, even one about groupies.

Lauren had sat motionless for *that* answer, pretending to study her apple cider, her fingers gripping the sweating glass, her heart doing its damndest to thump its way into her throat. It had been there so much since Nick returned she suspected the deluded organ believed that's where it was meant to be.

"Groupies are like chocolate, Josh," Nick said, mirth still threading through his words. His eyes however... Lauren could feel them on her, serious and contemplative. "A stupid man will think he can gorge himself on them with no consequences. But then he turns around and discovers they're just empty calories. They've just messed up his life when the only thing good for him was what he'd already been eating all along."

Josh raised his eyebrows, the action so like Nick's that Lauren's belly clenched. "And what's that?" Josh asked, voice almost a bated breath.

Nick held up the last of his lunch. "Toasted cheese and Vegemite sandwiches," he answered and popped the final corner into his mouth with a grin.

Lauren wasn't surprised to see Josh was utterly, completely enthralled. So much so, that when Rhys called and asked him to come over for a game of Rock Band, he said no. She'd never known her son to turn down his best friend. It should have petrified her. It didn't. It made her heart sing. And her soul weep. Even more so when Nick rose to his feet, gathered up the dirty dishes and began washing them in the sink.

Finally, Aslin returned, the bodyguard moving about Lauren's small kitchen like the proverbial bull doing his best to keep the proverbial china shop accident and breakage free. "Got rid of Holston," he said, lowering himself into the last seat at the table. "Although I don't think he likes me much anymore."

Nick laughed and Josh asked what Aslin had done. Lauren found herself warmed by such contented enjoyment that she stopped breathing for a second, her heart stilling. And then Nick smiled at her, just a simple smile, and it started again. Fast. Hard.

It was too much. Too much to take. Too much to comprehend, and she'd turned her back on the disquieting scene. Now, here she stood at the counter, her back to them all, trying to steady her heart's rapid beat with slow, steady breaths in the guise of making a cheese sandwich without the Vegemite for Aslin.

"How do you think he knew you were here, Nick?"

It was Josh who asked the question, his voice part awe, part consternation. Lauren pulled another steadying breath. Her son was falling under Nick's easy charm and the excitement of his celebrity. How did she return life to normal after this?

You can't. You know that. You know that and a part of you doesn't want to. A bigger part than you would have yourself believe. And you know that as well.

"I'm guessing it was someone at the pub last night." A relaxed humour threaded through Nick's answer. "Most in there seemed like locals, but I must admit, the barkeeper didn't look like it."

"He's not. He's from Tamworth. He moved here a year ago. Asked Mum out a couple of times."

Lauren scrunched up her face, giving up any hope of slowing her heart. Of course Josh would have to reveal *that* little tidbit of information.

"And what did your mum say?" Nick asked, the laugh in his voice sounding over emphasised. She closed her eyes. Just what she needed, a jealous rock star.

"No," Josh answered. "Even when he asked if she wanted to go to your latest concert in Sydney. He bought tickets and everything."

"The concert I haven't done yet? The one that's only just gone on sale? The one that doesn't happen until March next year?"

Josh laughed. "That's the one."

"The tickets to that only went on sale, what, three days ago, am I right, Aslin?"

"That's right, Nick."

There was a pause. "So this bloke asked your mum out three days ago?"

Lauren heard Josh chuckle. "Yep."

"And she said no."

"Yep."

"What do you think she'd say if I asked her to the concert?"

Try as hard as she might, Lauren couldn't stop the grin pulling at her lips. She turned, leaning against the counter with Aslin's sandwich held out before her. "I think she'd say maybe."

Nick smiled up at her, his wholly kissable lips curling, his eyes telling her quite clearly what he thought of her maybe. Her stomach did a nice little flip-flop thingy at the heated intensity in his gaze. Her sex did a nice little fluttering thingy too. And her nipples got tight. She licked her lips. Oh boy, she was insane.

"Josh?" Aslin suddenly asked, and Lauren blinked, the hypnotic pull of Nick's complete attention shattered by the bodyguard's clipped, strong voice. "Have you been in a helicopter before?"

Josh pulled his patented are-you-kidding face, the kind

119

reserved for questions from adults all teenagers knew to be pointless. "No."

Aslin gave him a nonchalant look. "Would you like to?"

The question hadn't finished before Josh was on his feet, staring at Lauren with an open-mouthed excitement she hadn't seen since...well, since he'd discovered Nick Blackthorne in his home. "Can I, Mum? Please?"

Her belly twisted again. If she said yes, did that mean she would be left alone with Nick? Would she be strong enough to resist him, to resist herself, if that was the case?

"What about your friend—Rhys, is it? Would he like to go too?" Nick asked, enjoying his son's happiness.

If possible, Josh's mouth fell farther open. "Are you fucking—I mean, are you serious?" He held out his hands to Lauren, his face beseeching her as only a teenage boy can do. "Mum? Ya gotta say yes? Please? Please?"

Nick's bodyguard turned to her, a smile she could have sworn was conniving on his menacingly handsome face. "It'll only be a couple of hours, Ms. Robbins. And I'm a fully licensed pilot. He'll be safe, I promise."

She swallowed, her mouth suddenly dry.

"Aslin's an ex-British SAS commando, Lauren," Nick piped up, his body loose and relaxed in his seat. "I trust him with my life every day." His eyes grew serious. "And I'll trust him with Josh's as well. Every day. Any time."

The significance of the last part of his statement wasn't lost on Lauren. Nick was telling her—and Josh, even though Josh didn't know it—that Josh's safety was equally as important as his own. And that as far as Nick was concerned, now part of his responsibility.

A heavy vice wrapped around her chest and squeezed. God, she should be furious about that. She should be, but she wasn't. Truth be known, she had no bloody clue how she felt.

Messed up, Lauren. Messed up, confused and petrified. And horny. So bloody horny since Nick showed up.

"Mum?"

It was the desperate note in Josh's voice that undid her. The small-town kid given a chance to experience something completely outside his known world and half-convinced his mother was going to ruin it all.

She fixed him with a stern stare. "Okay, but—" She had to stop and wait for him to finish making whooping noises and jumping around the kitchen. "But Mr. Rhodes is in charge and he has my full permission to break you in two if you don't behave."

"I will." He laughed, still leaping around the small room. "I mean, I won't, I won't."

She let out a sigh. "Try not to fall out of the thing, okay?"

Josh did something totally unexpected then. He grabbed her in a bone-crunching hug and gave her a kiss on the cheek. "You're bloody brilliant, Mum."

"That she is," Nick murmured, his gaze on her face. Lauren doubted Josh heard him. He was too busy grinning and bombarding Aslin with questions about the flight, the most important being when?

The massive man swallowed the last of his sandwich and then rose to his feet. "How's now sound?"

"Epic."

Lauren's pulse leapt into overdrive. Now? She wasn't ready. She wasn't...

But it was too late. Before she could utter another word, Josh was digging his mobile out of his jeans' pocket and running for the front door. "Rhys, get your arse to the helicopter. Now!"

Aslin laughed. So did Nick, but to Lauren's ears it sounded strained, as if he was just as on edge about the approaching situation as she.

Nervous? Why the hell was she nervous?

She licked her lips, her mouth dry. She watched Aslin nod to Nick, a single nod that seemed to speak volumes. Nick nodded back, and then the bodyguard was gone, leaving her along with her ex.

Her heart thumped harder in her chest.

"You should have told me, Lauren."

His reproach was soft and gentle, as was his gaze. Not what she expected at all. But then, the Nick that had come back to Murriundah wasn't the Nick who had left her in Sydney. There was something different about him, and it wasn't just the age in his face. Something...deeper. She frowned, wrapping her arms around her ribcage. Her legs were cold, her toes the same. That had to be why her nipples were tight and her breath shallow. It had nothing to do with the confusion knotting in her belly.

"You should have told me," he repeated, not moving from where he stood on the other side of the table.

She licked her lips again. "And what would you have done, Nick? Come back? Given up your new life, your new world? I can't see you working in an office, can you? Or packing shelves to pay for nappies and doctors' appointments?"

A flicker of darkness flared in his eyes. "You didn't give me that chance, did you?"

Lauren's stomach churned. She hadn't. At the time she was convinced she was doing the right thing. She still thought she had...didn't she?

His gaze didn't waver from her eyes. "Did you know you were pregnant when I..." He didn't finish the question. So she did for him.

"When you left me? When you decided the lure of being a rock star was more powerful than the lure of being us?" She shook her head. "No."

A short breath left him and he scrubbed at his face with hands that looked like they were shaking. Another difference in the man she'd known since he was fourteen. The Nick Blackthorne she'd fallen in love with all those years ago would never show any sign of weakness. He'd worn cocky confidence the same way most people wore their clothes. It had been part of his charm, part of the reason why she'd fallen so hard for him, and she'd grown to hate it toward the end. Now that cockiness didn't seem to exist, not the way it had before. He was still Nick, still arrogant, but that cockiness was tempered with what she'd thought was maturity. Perhaps it was something else though. Something she couldn't understand?

No. You're just making excuses, Lauren. You want him so much. You want the fantasy he's offering so much you're willing to believe he's changed. And you'll find yourself exactly where you did fifteen years ago—broken and empty and wounded.

She hugged herself tighter, her throat thick.

Nick dropped his hands from his face, staring at her across the table. The smell of toasted bread hung on the air, a smell she'd once enjoyed, a smell that always brought with it memories of laughter and contentedness and sensual passion. God, how deluded could she be?

"You should have told me, Lauren. I had a right to know. Josh had a right to know. *Has* a right."

She ground her teeth, the mention of her son like a knife in her chest. She'd never told Josh who his father was and he'd stopped asking. "A mistake in my past," she'd called Nick.

"You left me, Nick," she said, voice husky. "The fame, the

fans, the groupies, hordes of women throwing themselves at you, recording producers procuring for you anything you wanted...I couldn't compete with that." She let out a sigh, her gaze jumping around her kitchen. Her small, homey, far-from-modern kitchen with its clutter and temperamental microwave. So far removed from the kind of kitchen an international award-winning performer would own.

She returned her stare to Nick. "Being a star, being a musician, was all you ever wanted, all you ever loved. Being a father wouldn't have fit into those plans at all."

His nostrils flared. "You're wrong, Lauren. I loved you too."

She shook her head. "Not enough, Nick. Not enough to stop you walking out on me."

He didn't answer her. What did she expect him to say? There wasn't anything to say, was there? She had to think with her head. Her head, not her heart. And her head knew as much as she ached for him, loved him, there wasn't a hope in hell of there being a happy-ever-after in this. Just another song, perhaps? Another song that would sting her eyes with tears whenever she heard him sing it on the radio.

Another sigh welled up in her chest. "I'm going to have a shower. I think two p.m. is late enough to still be wearing pyjamas, don't you?" She snorted, looking down at herself. "Well, half-wearing pyjamas."

Before he could say anything, she turned and walked from the kitchen. He didn't reach for her as she passed him. He didn't call after her.

Swinging the bathroom door shut behind her, she stripped herself of her shirt. A chill rippled over her, the tiled room's cool air like a million icy kisses on her flushed skin. And it *was* flushed. For all the wretched confessions and arguments she presented, her body was still more turned on, more aroused by

Nick than any man she'd ever known. He may have hurt her beyond measure fifteen years ago, but he'd branded her his as well. In so many ways, none the least with the boy who looked and behaved so much like him.

She closed her eyes, fighting the tears. She wouldn't cry. She wouldn't.

The water was freezing when she first turned it on, the pipes outside no doubt wrapped in winter. She considered stepping into it. Surely that would shock her back to rational behavior?

"Idiot," she muttered, twisting open the hot faucet. All that would achieve would be her getting a cold and then she'd be miserable *and* snotty.

A moment later she stood under the warm stream of water, head down, letting it pour over her. It flowed over her cheeks, followed the line of her parted lips. It trickled down the back of her neck, down the curve of her breasts, over her puckered nipples. She pressed her palms to the cubicle wall, the tiles cool against her skin, and closed her eyes. Tears rolled from them, washed away by the shower's warm caress that took the salty drops with it down her body, over her belly, past her navel to the curve of her sex.

Between her thighs. Over her sex.

And the whole time, silent tears leaked from her eyes and her heart cried for Nick. Nick, damn him. Nick.

Her shower screen slid open and he stood on the other side, his nostrils flaring, his jaw bunched.

"I'm sorry."

His voice was roughened. Nothing more than a low whisper.

Palms still pressed to the wall, she stared back at him. Her breasts grew round with want even as her throat grew tight. "I hate you, Nick."

"No, you don't."

She closed her eyes, the water licking away her tears before they could slip from her lashes. "No, damn you." She lifted her head and gazed at him. "I don't."

Without a word, he curled his fingers under the hem of his shirt, pulled it up over his head and stepped into the shower.

She turned to him, instantly and immediately, and slid her hands up his chest, over his hard nipples before twining her arms around his neck and pulling his mouth down to hers.

The kiss was beyond her. She was no more in control of her body than she was her heart. All she knew was at that very moment there was nothing else in the world she wanted more than to feel Nick against her, holding her, inside her. It was foolish and stupid and weak, but too powerful to resist. She wanted him. He was the only one to ever make her feel whole. The only one ever to make her feel cherished. For all the pain he'd brought to her world, he'd also given her more happiness and love than she could remember. Right now, in this shower, he was Nick. *Her* Nick. Not the world's Nick. Not the record producers' Nick. Hers. And she would lose herself in her Nick and deal with the pain of the stolen moment after he'd returned to the world again.

She stroked his tongue with hers, loving the way his arms held her firmly to his body. The water flowed over them both, joining their kiss, slicking their flesh. She pressed herself closer to him, the sensation of her wet breasts sliding against his wet chest too erotic. A moan vibrated low in her throat, or was it in Nick's? She couldn't tell. Didn't care. Rising on to tiptoes, she rolled her hips, an unspoken request for that still trapped in his sodden jeans. Lord, she wanted him inside her. Wanted him filling her, stretching her. Possessing her.

Like a junkie wanted a hit.

Head swimming, she dragged one hand down his torso, her lips still drinking from his as she fumbled with his fly. He stopped her, his fingers replacing hers to deftly release the top button. His erection strained at his zipper and Lauren scraped her thumb over its emerging tip.

He groaned, pulling from the kiss long enough to sear a path over her jaw line, up to her ear. He caught her earlobe with his teeth, nipping with almost painful force before sucking it into his mouth, all the while tugging his fly open.

His cock finally sprung free, a long, thick rod Lauren immediately captured with her fingers. He moaned, the sound raw and urgent, his shaft convulsing in her hand. One throbbing pulse, then another, another.

"Oh, Nick." She swept her thumb over its tip again, the warm water from the shower turning its velvet-smooth head to a slick dome. "You have the most amazing dick."

He laughed at her brazen claim, cupping her left breast and giving it a gentle squeeze. "And you have the most amazing breasts," he murmured, lifting his head. His eyes were heavy-lidded, his thick black lashes spiky with water.

She arched her back a little, pushing her breast forward as she pumped his cock once, twice. "Hmmm, I think I remember you mentioning that a few times."

He chuckled. "Possibly. In fact I think I wrote a song about your breasts once. *Twin worlds of heaven within my grasp,"* he crooned, kneading his fingers against the heavy swell of her flesh, *"within my reach, I want to suck them, fuck them. Fuck, do I want to suck them, fuck them."*

Lauren laughed, the words making her pussy flutter. She squeezed his cock, unable to miss how thicker and harder it was growing in her hand. "Don't remember hearing that one in the charts."

He grinned, drops of water trickling over his lips. As insane as it was, Lauren felt jealous of those drops. "They wouldn't let me record it. Said it was too dirty."

Her sex constricted again. The feel of his thumb swirling patterns over her nipple sent ribbons of delicious heat into her core. "Spoil sports," she panted.

"Ain't that right."

Before she could come back with something witty, because witty was pretty much beyond her at this point, he bowed his body and closed his lips over her nipple. She gasped, tangling the fingers of her free hand in his wet hair. The shower spray streamed over her chest as he suckled on her breast. His cock pulsed in her fingers, the metal teeth of his fly scraping at her knuckles as she sought to keep him in her grip, to squeeze him tighter.

Want him naked. Want him—

He dropped into a crouch, sucking with ferocious hunger on first one breast then the other, his hands roaming her belly, her waist, her hips. She trembled, closing her eyes against the water pouring over her. Or was it the pleasure rolling through her?

When his hands found their way to her pussy, when his thumb stroked over her clit, she knew she had to stop him. She was too close, too close. Too close and too desperate for him.

"Nick." She pushed him away, smiling at him as he frowned up at her. "I want you in my mouth. Before the hot water runs out, I want you in my mouth."

His eyes dilated. His nostrils flared. Without a word, he rose to his feet, every muscle in his torso coiled, his skin flushed with heat. He gazed at her, Adam's apple jerking up and down his throat. "It won't take long, babe," he murmured, a faint pink painting his cheeks. "Not with your lips on my dick, your tongue. I won't be able to hold on for—"

She didn't let him finish. She sank to her knees, yanked his jeans' saturated, clinging waistline down over his hips, his arse, his thighs, and took his solid, turgid length in her mouth.

Chapter Nine

Jesus fucking Christ, he was going to die.

Nick threw back his head, staring wildly at the bathroom's white ceiling. Steam swirled above his head, tiny particles of water that danced with lazy rhythm. He stared with blank rapture at them, fighting the pleasure Lauren wrought on his body, struggling to stop the orgasm threatening to unleash itself with seismic force from his very fucking soul.

Jesus. Lauren was giving him head. Lauren was giving him head in her shower.

The frenzied, heady thought sent fresh tension into his groin. His balls swelled, pressing high on his inner thighs, aching for release. His cock convulsed in Lauren's mouth and his hips bucked forward, an involuntary action he could no more control than repress. Christ, he was going to come any moment now. He was going to fucking blow his load with barely five sucking strokes of Lauren's mouth and tongue.

"Babe," he groaned, fisting his hands in her hair. "I'm...I'm not...if you..." The rest of his choked confession was lost to a groan as Lauren's fingers found his sac. She tugged, a barely there pressure that sent shards of exquisite heat into his core. He bucked again, squeezing his eyes shut, his breath hissing through his clenched teeth.

She sucked on his length, taking him deeper and deeper

into her mouth until he pushed at the back of her throat. And then with a gentle tug of his balls, she slid back up his length. Her tongue laved his cock as she went, long steady strokes until her lips wrapped the ridge of its domed head. Until her teeth scraped at its very tip before she plunged down his erection once again. Deeper this time. So deep. So deep.

"Fuck... that's good... so good... babe... that's... that's... so... fuck..." His moans rose in the cubicle like the swirling steam, a mindless song far more primal than any he'd sung before. His knees quivered, his body rapidly succumbing to the concentrated pleasure of Lauren's mouth. So close. The base of his spine tingled. His ragged breath burned in his lungs like fire. Christ, how had he lasted this long?

Because it's Lauren. Lauren who knows how to play your body as well as you know how to play the guitar. Lauren, who always did. Who always did, and now you'll never want anyone but her ever again. Just Lauren, just...

"Lauren," he moaned, her name on his lips pushing him over the edge, propelling him into an orgasm he couldn't resist anymore. A crescendo of sensations, of wants, of needs, of pleasure. He came, his orgasm erupting from his balls, pouring through his cock, through his soul, into Lauren's mouth. She swallowed thick spurts of release with fierce hunger, her own moans rising to his ears, vibrating through his shaft. He bucked into her, thrust into her, pumped into her mouth until rhythm ceased to exist to him and his body was no longer his, but hers. Until his seed was drained of him, and her tongue washed him clean.

Until he was lost to her. Christ, he was lost to her.

His heart hammered in his chest, his throat, his ears. He stood motionless. No, not motionless. His chest was rising and falling so fast anyone would think he'd just run a marathon. And his cock kept pulsing in tiny jerks, the fading beat of his orgasm still in possession of his dick. As was Lauren. Her lips no longer wrapped his shaft, but her fingers had replaced them, holding him with a gentle pressure. Held him, touched him. He looked down at her, his lips parting as he watched her lean forward and lick the last bead of his release from his cock.

It was too much. He was too spent. A wild convulsion rocked through him and he laughed, a choked exhalation of breath. "N-no more. I can't..."

She lifted her eyes to his, her tongue slipping out of her mouth to slowly swipe at the corner of her lips, the water from the shower flowing over her, dripping from her puckered nipples.

"You drive me crazy, Lauren Robbins," he uttered on a wobbly breath.

She traced the treble cleft tattoo on his lower abdomen with one slow, steady finger. "You drive me mental, Nick Blackthorne."

Her answer sent a wave of sheer happiness through him. He laughed. "At least the hot water didn't run out. Might have been a touch embarrassing if I was suddenly standing in cold water."

She grinned, rising to her feet to stand before him. "I doubt the cold water would have made any difference."

It wasn't at all possible—he was too drained—but his groin throbbed with delight at her response anyways. It throbbed with an interest, a need he knew he'd never quench.

He leant toward her, letting his chest brush her nipples as he reached behind her and killed the water. "You realize it's my turn now, yes?"

She laughed, a throaty sound that made his groin stir again. "You think you have it in you?"

He snaked one hand up her wet body to cup her breast and

rasp his thumb over her hardened nipple. "Oh, I may not be a spring chicken anymore, but I'm pretty fucking certain I can bring you to climax again and again while this old body of mine recovers."

She leant into his kneading hand. "Prove it."

He shucked his legs out of his wet jeans, not an easy task to do while still in the shower cubicle. Even more difficult when his attention was fixed so firmly on Lauren as she walked across the bathroom floor. Her lush body still glistened with water, her arse cheeks bunching and stretching with sublime perfection every step she took. She paused, looking at him over her shoulder as she reached for a fluffy bottle-green towel and wrapped it around her body. "Coming?"

"You fucking better believe it," he muttered, fighting with the last leg of his jeans as it clung to his foot with possessive force.

Lauren was out of the bathroom by the time he won the battle, and he all but sprinted from the room, pausing in the hallway for a brief second, water dripping from him. Shit, he didn't know where her bedroom was.

A faint scratching noise pricked his ears from the right, and he turned and hurried toward the open door five metres away. Someone striking a match. That's what the sound was. Someone striking a match followed by the distinct crackle as tinder took flame.

He entered the room, noticing three things at once. There was a fire beginning to build in the small brick fireplace on the wall to his left, the room smelt like its owner, clean and delicate and flowery, and Lauren lay stretched on the bed. Naked.

His heart slammed harder against his chest and his cock twitched again. At this rate, it wouldn't take long at all before he would be sliding into her. Jesus, just *looking* at her turned him on. Turned him on and left him at her mercy. No, that wasn't right. Left him...absolute. Without her in his life, he'd been insubstantial. A rock star who made his career singing of love. A man who'd stupidly abandoned it when he thought there was more to be had. Without her he had the word, but not the meaning. Without her, the rhythm of his life was wrong.

He would never abandon her again.

Ever. He'd once thought he needed to sing to live. He was wrong. He hadn't been living all these years. He'd been existing. Just existing. The only time he'd lived had been with Lauren. In her arms, in her heart. And now that he was with her it wasn't music he heard, but words. Three words. I love her.

He crossed the room.

She watched him come, her lips curling into a small smile, her gaze half-lidded. He climbed onto the end of the bed, curling his fingers around her ankles with a feather-light grip. A shiver rippled through her, an almost inaudible intake of breath slipping past her lips. He slowly spread her legs, his stare holding hers. She pulled another breath, her breasts rising as she did so. He dropped his gaze to them for a moment, reveling in the puckered tautness of her nipples, before returning to her face. For a surreal moment he remembered the day the video clip for "Night Whispers" had been shot. He'd been on set, a derelict building in Brooklyn crawling with film crew and musicians, and Lauren had walked towards him through a plume of dry ice mist.

He remembered his heart slamming into his throat. He remembered his balls contracting, his dick stiffening, and then the mist swirled away and he realized it wasn't Lauren. It had been the actress the director had cast as the nameless lover Nick was singing about. He'd lost himself in a bottle of Chivas that night, and tried to lose himself deeper in the woman that wasn't Lauren. But after a minute with her lips on his flesh he'd known it was a joke. A fucking joke, and he'd sent her from his New York apartment and fallen asleep to the sound of "Night Whispers" playing *ad infinitum* from the speakers embedded in the walls of his room.

But the Lauren on the bed before him now was the real Lauren. Her beauty natural and ethereal, not created by a team of makeup artists and cosmetic surgeons. Her smile reached her eyes, eyes shining with passion for life, not a predatory gleam. Her warmth, her humor, her intelligence...everything uniquely Lauren. And the real Lauren was watching him now, longing and desire and want burning in her eyes. For him.

His head swam and his balls throbbed. His Lauren. His heart. His goddess.

He lowered his head to her calf and pressed his lips to the smooth curve of fine muscle. He touched his tongue to her skin, feeling the tremble in her body through his hands. With slow strokes, he licked his way up her leg, bending it enough to explore the delicious back of her knee before straightening it completely and resting it against his chest. He stared down into her face, loving the way she watched him through lowered lashes. Her lips parted, her breasts rising and falling with shallow, shaky breaths. Holding her leg upright, he inched himself farther up the bed, drawing his groin closer to her pussy. She moaned, her hands moving to her belly. His throat thickened, his pulse kicking up a notch as she dipped her fingers to her sex.

Oh, boy...

He'd watched Lauren play with herself before. She'd tease him sometimes in their small Sydney apartment. Had strutted through the living room buck naked, her fingers skimming her nipples as she threw him flirty looks over her shoulder. Had stroked at the trim darkness of her pubic hair as she waited for him to climb onto their bed. Never had she entered her own heat with her fingers like she did now with slow, deliberate penetrations accompanying low, breathless whimpers. Slow, deliberate penetrations followed by just as slow withdrawals, her fingers leaving her folds glistening with her juices. Fingers she rose to her lips and touched with her tongue.

Nick's head swam.

The sight was so fucking arousing.

The smile of a sex goddess—*his* sex goddess—curled Lauren's lips. "Do you want to lick my fingers, Nick?"

He growled, threw her leg aside and captured her offered fingers with his mouth. Her taste coated his tongue, exploded in his brain. He sucked at her fingers, holding her hand with both of his. His cock jerked, her taste on his tongue, her musk in his breath, her heat against his thighs were all too intoxicating. She closed her eyes and moaned, her other hand smoothing over her breasts, pinching at her nipples. His cock pulsed again, and again when she slowly inched that hand down over her belly to her pussy, replacing the fingers he now sucked in his mouth.

Jesus, Nick. She's made you hard already.

She had. She fucked herself with her fingers, her soft moans of pleasure the most evocative song he'd ever heard, and made him hard.

So hard.

Hard enough to bury himself in her sex.

He did. He removed her hand from her pussy and sank his length, once again fully engorged, into her in one single thrust.

"Lord, that's so fucking good." The raw cry ripped from her. She arched on the bed, wrapping her legs around his hips. Her heels drove into his butt cheeks, pushing him deeper, deeper inside her. He pumped into her, one hand gripping the duvet beside her head, the other kneading her breast. She was tight, so wonderfully tight and wet. Her inner muscles squeezed his

136

length, holding it with forceful possession as he thrust in and out of her. Her nails scraped at his back, raked at his shoulders, and suddenly, with a wicked groan, she was rolling him onto his back, straddling his hips and taking him deeper still. So deep, so deep.

She leant forward, brushed her breasts over his lips and pulled back when he tried to catch one nipple with his mouth, a throaty chuckle vibrating through her as she did so. He felt the laugh thrum around his straining cock, the sensation sending fresh blood to his dick. His balls ached. Christ, he didn't think he'd get it up again so soon, and here he was on the verge of blowing his load already?

"Goddess," he rasped, running his hands over her hips, up her legs.

"Lover," she whispered back, threading the fingers of her right hand through the fingers of his left and moving his hand to her breast. It was heavy and swollen and ripe with desire. He scraped his thumb over her nipple, loving the way she closed her eyes and hummed in appreciation. He loved that she was in charge. He loved how she took pleasure from his body with such confident leisure. He loved how she squeezed her innermost muscles in pulse after deliberate, exquisite pulse as she rode his length. He loved how he was just that to her, her lover, not Nick Blackthorne rock star, but just the man she gave her body, her heart, her soul to. He loved her. Everything about her.

"Fuck, I need you, babe," he groaned, rolling his hips upward, thrusting deeper into her heat.

"Like a rhythm," she murmured, eyes fluttering closed, back arching into his penetration. "Like a curse."

And with those words her orgasm detonated in her core. Shuddered through her. Made her pussy contract and her cream flow. She opened her eyes and gazed down into his face, her orgasm gripping him, squeezing him until—with the words to "Gotta Run" whispering through his head—he surrendered to his own climax and pumped his seed into her with spurt after spurt after spurt.

"Goddess," he rasped again. Or maybe he cried it. He wasn't sure. He didn't care. His body wasn't his anymore. It was hers, Lauren's, and he wanted it no other way. No other way.

Eventually, the convulsions of pleasure rocking them both subsided, and she slumped against Nick's chest, his cock still wonderfully buried in her still-pulsing heat, and rested her cheek on his shoulder.

He smoothed his hands over the length of her back, up to her nape and back down to her hips. "I love you, Lauren." He whispered the words against the top of her head, incapable of keeping them in his soul any longer. "Marry me?"

She didn't answer.

A cold beat thumped in his temple. He swallowed, a heavy knot twisting in his gut. The words formed on his lips again, but he bit them back. She'd heard him. He could feel it in the way her body grew still. He slid a hand to her chin and tucked his fingers under it.

"Don't, Nick," she murmured, refusing to let him raise her face to his.

"Surely you can't think I'm going to walk away from you again? Not after this?"

"What's so different from what we had before?"

He swallowed, his stare jerking around her ceiling. He could feel her heart pounding in her chest. It struck his through the perfection of her breast with such force he didn't know whose beat was whose. "I'm not leaving you, Lauren. You can't tell me this wasn't...this *isn't* the way it's meant to be. You can't. And if you do, you're lying."

"When you came to me in the shower, I allowed myself this one moment." Her breath was warm on his chest as she spoke. "But that's all, Nick. I'm not strong enough to do it all over again, and I'd never expect you to give it all up. You'd grow to hate me if you did."

He tugged on her chin again, needing to see her eyes, but she refused to let him.

"What if I tell you I want to give it up?"

"Then *I'd* be the one calling *you* a liar." Her fingers drew small circles on his chest, and a part of Nick wondered if she even realized she was doing it. "Your Tropical Sin Tour concert tickets are already on sale. You're in the middle of recording your next album. Those aren't the actions of a man wanting to give it up."

He closed his eyes, his mouth dry. "They *are* the actions of a man who didn't realize the life he was living wasn't the life he wanted though."

She laughed, a short sharp snort. That he was still embedded in her sex made the sound all the more incongruous. "You've changed, Nick. I'll give you that, but not that much."

"And you're the same, Lauren? I don't think so. The Lauren I fell in love with all those years ago would have given me, *us*, a chance. She wouldn't have kept a son a secret." He threaded his fingers in her hair, wishing to fuck she'd look at him.

She moved, slowly rising away from his chest until she supported herself on her elbows and studied his face. "*That* Lauren didn't have another living soul to care for, Nick. To protect. That changes everything. You can't understand."

The shift in her position made him all too aware he'd yet to withdraw from her sheath. That his cock, still semi-hard from their passion, was nestled within her wet heat. It was surreal.

Surreal and terrifying at once. This may be the last time she let him make love to her and he couldn't think of a more soul-aching end.

Then don't let it end. Fight for her. Fight for this.

Nick's head swam. He squeezed his eyes. Fisted his hands. "There's an article in next month's *Rolling Stone*—" he felt her stiffen at his abrupt change in topic, "—written by McKenzie Wood, a journalist I know very well. The woman whose wedding I came here to ask you to attend with me."

Her eyes narrowed. "What's this got to do with us? With your...your proposal?"

He gave her a wry smile. "The article is an exclusive story about me." He paused, long enough to pull a steadying breath. He hadn't talked about the events of his life that changed him so much since the day he'd revealed it all to McKenzie and Aidan, almost nine months ago. It was still raw. Still...unsettling. But he needed Lauren to understand. If he stood any chance of the future he longed for with every fibre in his being, he needed her to understand. "My parents died two years ago, did you know that?"

She nodded, her eyebrows dipping. "In that car accident on the F3. It was all over the news, along with footage of the wreckage and you arriving back in Australia. I went to the funeral. I saw you grieving."

He blinked. "I didn't know that."

She lowered her eyelids and turned her head aside. "I didn't want you to. And I am sorry for your loss. I'm sorry it's also taken two years for me to say that to you. They were lovely people. I missed them when they moved back to Sydney."

"When they were killed, I learned I was adopted."

Lauren gasped. Her eyes snapped open, her stare on his face. "Nick, I didn't...why didn't you..."

He smoothed a hand up her arm, drawing strength from her warmth. A warmth he'd stupidly denied himself for a lifetime. "I discovered I was adopted and that I had a younger brother," he continued, needing to get it out as much as he needed her. "It took me a long time to find him, and when I did he was in a messed-up state, suffering from abuse both physical and emotional his whole life. Eight months after I met Derek, after I'd begun to form a relationship with him, the brother I never knew I had, he committed suicide."

Lauren was still, her face etched in shocked pain. She stared at him, wordless, her heat seeping into the sudden cold wanting to claim his heart.

"So the family that wasn't really mine was taken away from me, and the family I never knew I had was denied me. Kinda fucks you up a little. Well, it did me. I lost the music in my soul and it took two special people to help me find it again. But when I finally got my shit together I realised what I wanted more than anything else was to see you."

He swallowed, the tale done. There were more details, but he didn't want to share them now. Not now. Now he wanted to curl his arms around Lauren's waist, burying his face in the curve of her neck, breathe in the delicate fragrance of her scent, take *her* into his soul and just be. Be with the family he'd only just found, the family he wanted more than he could express.

He brushed her hair from her face, traced her lips with the pad of his thumb and gazed into her eyes. "I'm a man of words, babe, you know that. But there are no words for how much I want you in my life, want Josh in my life. No words. Just a pain in my heart that will know no relief until I hear your answer." He paused, traced her lips again before lowering his hand to his chest. "Whatever it may be."

Her gaze devoured his face. Her teeth caught her bottom lip. She shifted her position, enough that his spent cock, finally flaccid, slipped from her sex. The loss of such a physical, intimate connection rocked him, but he didn't move to halt her. As much as he wanted to, he didn't.

She shifted her hips, her legs over his, her palms coming to rest on his chest. Over his heart. Closing her eyes, she drew a slow breath, her eyebrows dipping as if she fought a battle he couldn't see.

"I can't say yes, Nick."

Her answer was a whisper. A whisper that sheared through him like a molten blade.

"I can't," she went on, her voice still barely a breath. "Not yet. But I can say maybe."

He whooped. A fair dinkum whoop. Bursting out laughing, he wrapped his arms around her and rolled her on to her back, smiling down at her as waves of glee flowed over him. Maybe. Maybe.

She laughed, a nervous chuckle that made his heart beat faster. "You did hear me correctly, didn't you?" She cupped her hand to the side of his face, a confused frown creasing her forehead. "I didn't say yes. I said maybe. I need a few days, a few weeks. I need to think. I need to—"

He grinned and stole a quick kiss before laughing once again. "A maybe isn't a no, babe, and it sure isn't a 'fuck off, Blackthorne'."

He claimed her mouth, unable not to. He kissed her, smiling as he did so, and at some stage his hands found her hips, her breasts. At some stage her thighs straddled his hips and she was impaled on his length again, moving up and down his dick, his eager, hungry, rigid dick, and even the word yes meant nothing compared to the sensation of being inside her.

And when they both came, long moments later, their skin slicked with perspiration, their breaths shallow, their fingers entwined, he swore the *yes* that tore from her lips in a raw cry over and over again was the most magical word he'd ever heard.

But not as magical as the words, "Mum, we're home!"

Those three magical words, hollered by Josh moments after their climax, had the power to send both he and Lauren scrambling out of bed in a wild thrashing of arms and legs.

"It was so freaking awesome," Josh called, somewhere in the house. "Rhys almost threw up and—"

She stumbled backward, frantically searching her room. "Clothes," she hissed. "Where the hell are my—oh God, your jeans are still in the shower."

He tried not to laugh. He truly did. But the laugh left him anyway, deep chuckles that vibrated low in his chest. Right before Lauren threw a pillow at him.

"—Aslin buzzed Mr. McGimmon's house—" Josh's voice wafted down the hallway, louder this time, "—who was on his back porch making out with Mrs. Bailey and we fucking—I mean freaking *flew* all the way to freaking Newcastle and back and—"

"Get dressed," Lauren mouthed at him, tugging her legs into a pair of faded jeans she pulled from the top of a neatly folded stack of clothes on a chair beside the bed.

"In what?" he mouthed back.

"Aslin says he'll take us on another ride tomorrow if that's okay with you," Josh's voice was close enough now Nick could hear the faint cracking on the higher inflections.

"Here," Lauren snatched something black from the same stack of clothes, "they're Josh's. They might fit—"

"Mum? Where are you?" Josh called. Nick's heart leapt into his throat. His son was no longer recounting his helicopter ride from the foyer or front of the house. He was almost at the bedroom. Close. "Are you—"

"Nick?" Aslin's thunderous rumble had Lauren glaring at him, a second before she yanked a T-shirt from the stack and pulled it over her head. An image of Optimus Prime stretched over her glorious, unrestrained breasts, her nipples poking at Nick through the T-shirt's soft black cotton.

"Miss Robbins?" a new voice called, a voice cracking far more than Josh's and far higher in pitch.

"Oh, you've got to be kidding me." Lauren groaned. "Rhys?"

Nick felt his eyebrows shoot up his forehead. "Rhys?"

Lauren glared at him some more, sprinted from the room only to return a second later with the shirt he'd discarded in the bathroom. "Why the hell aren't you dressed yet?"

"Mum?"

"Miss Robbins?"

Nick flapped out the sweat pants Lauren had flung at him and shoved his left leg in. They were too short, but only a little.

"Hurry," Lauren mouthed, raking her fingers through her hair. It was an exercise in futility in Nick's opinion. The moment she'd exited the shower he'd been on her like white on rice, and now her hair looked like a fabulous, wild tumble of untamed curls and waves. Bed hair in its truest definition.

"Mum?" Josh called again.

Closer. So close Nick swore he smelt his son's deodorant.

With one last desperate rake at her hair, Lauren hurried across her bedroom and stepped out into the hallway. "I called back to you, Josh," Nick heard her say. "Are you deaf? Didn't you wear headphones? I was packing away the ironing."

There was a pause, followed by Josh saying, "Oh. All right. Where's Nick?"

"In the loo," Lauren answered and Nick had to bite his tongue to stop laughing. "What? Rock stars aren't allowed to pee like the rest of us?"

"Gross, Mum."

"Yeah, that's pretty filthy, Miss Robbins."

"Yeah, yeah, you'd know, Rhys. Does your mum know you're here?"

Nick heard Josh's best friend mumble something and then their footfalls echoed down the hallway, away from Lauren's bedroom.

He stood still for a long second, listening. For what, he wasn't sure. Whatever it was, he didn't want Josh to find him in Lauren's room. Now, where the hell was the loo? And if he flushed it, would Josh hear it wherever in the house Lauren had led the boys?

"Coast is clear."

It was Aslin's voice Nick heard just outside the doorway, a decidedly laughing note to his British accent.

"And the toilet is across the hall, door next to the bathroom. Just in case you're quizzed."

Nick stepped out of Lauren's bedroom, giving his bodyguard a wide grin.

Aslin cocked an eyebrow back. "Nice trousers."

Nick chuckled, beginning to walk down the hallway. "How was the ride?"

Aslin cast him a sidewards glance. "Josh is a great kid. Smart. Funny." He stopped walking and put his hand on Nick's arm. It was an uncommon move. Aslin was the closest thing to an uncle that Nick had, but he rarely touched Nick unless it was to protect him, or shield him from some over-zealous fan. Nick frowned up at him, something about the man's serious expression making his chest tight.

"Don't fuck it up, Nick. You can't walk away from this one.

If you do, you'll destroy three lives, not just your own."

"I'm not going to, mate. I love her. I never stopped. It just took me too fucking long to realise it."

"And now you do?"

Nick smiled. "I'm going to be a dad. And if she lets me, a husband."

He turned away from Aslin's stunned face, incapable of stopping the spring in his step. Rounding the entry way into the kitchen, he grinned at Josh and dropped into the empty seat beside the teenager.

"Holy shit, Josh!" the boy—Rhys—burst out, his eyes wide, his stare jerking backward and forward between Nick and Josh. "I always said you looked like Nick Blackthorne, but now you're in the same room together... Fuck, he could be your dad."

Chapter Ten

Lauren's stomach dropped. Her heart smacked into her throat. She stared at her son, her cheeks burning. Oh God, why did she have to blush? Why did her stupid face have to turn so red?

Words scrambled in her mind. Responses, deflections, all tumbling over one another.

"Dude," Rhys laughed, "Nick Blackthorne is wearing your tracky dacks."

Josh frowned, jerking his stare to Nick's legs, to Nick's face and then back to hers. "Mum, why is Nick wearing my tracksuit pants?"

She opened her mouth and heard Rhys say, "How long ago did you say your mum knew him?" Her son's best friend, a boy she'd watched grow up, a nice kid who always had a slightly skewed view of subtlety, laughed again. "I mean, seriously, check you both out."

Fire razed through Lauren's face. Josh slid his stare to Nick again, his jaw bunching, his throat working. His eyebrows pulled into a deeper frown and then he was looking at her once more, his eyes, so like his father's, unreadable.

"Rhys," she blurted, "I don't think—"

"How long ago *did* you know Nick, Mum?" Josh asked, his voice steady.

She swallowed. Flicked Nick another look. The room roared. Or maybe that was the blood in her ears? Her lips prickled. "Josh—" his name was a just a croak, "—this is...I-I...you need to..."

"Holy shit, dude," Rhys whispered. The awe-struck exclamation speared into Lauren's sanity like a blade of ice. "Nick Blackthorne is your *dad?*"

Josh shook his head, never taking his stare from Lauren. "No. Mum would have told me if that was the case, right, Mum?" He sucked in a breath, something in his face cutting into Lauren's soul. Something she never ever wanted to see in her son's eyes—accusation? Mistrust? Her heart tore.

"Josh..." she began.

He shook his head, stopping her. "If I was Nick Blackthorne's son you would have told me, right?"

She couldn't answer him. She couldn't. Lord, what did she say?

He jerked his stare, now wide-eyed, to Nick. "I mean, if I were your son...if you were my dad...she would have said something, would have told me, right? *Right?*"

Nick licked his lips, his jaw as tight as his son's. "Josh, we need to talk. Your mother...I..."

It was Nick's failure to deny it all that destroyed her son. Lauren could see that. She watched his shock, his pain and then his anger eat him up, his young face crumple under the revelation. Watched him shake his head, watched him stagger back a step. "This is bullshit. Bullshit."

Lauren's stomach rolled. She stepped toward him, reached for him. "Josh, please listen."

But he jerked away from her, his glare jumping from her to Nick and back to her again. And it was a glare, a dark, angry, baleful glare. "What? Wasn't I good enough to be Nick

Blackthorne's kid? Is that it? Did he pay you off? Did he pay you to shut up about me?"

"Dude," Rhys whispered, shocked disbelief turning the word to a groan.

"Josh." Nick made a move toward him but Josh hurried back another step, his hip colliding with the kitchen counter, his stare fixed on Lauren.

"And why's he here now then? Why the *fuck* is he standing in my home wearing my *fucking* tracksuit pants if *he's not my fucking father?*"

"Enough, Josh," Lauren snapped. Her gut rolled. Her breath tried to choke her. Oh Lord, this was her fault. All her fault.

"No, it's not enough, Mum." He stomped his foot on the floor. That baleful hurt still etched his face, turning it into a twisted mask. "How many times did I ask you who my dad was? How many? You never once thought you could tell me? I thought he was a prick, or that he hit you, or he was in prison. Shit, I thought he must be married to someone else. I grew up thinking all that kind of shit. Do you know how fucking hard it was going to school the week before Father's Day when I was little? When all the teachers had us kids make were Father's Day cards and presents? Do you know how fucking hard it was going to soccer and seeing everyone else's dads there?" He clenched his fists, pressed them to his face, his body shaking. "Jesus, Mum, do you know how fucking hard it was not having a dad to talk to when I had my first fucking wet dream? When I had to talk to you about it? Do you? And all this time I had a dad. I had a dad and you kept that from me?"

"Josh," Rhys said, shuffling a step forward, "dude, you're going to bust a valve."

Josh's face contorted. He turned away from them all,

thumped his fist against the counter. "Do you know how many times I lay awake at night pretending I had a dad? That he would walk in the door one day. And when he finally does, he's Nick fucking Blackthorne and he doesn't let on who he is at all."

Lauren's heart tore open. Josh's anguish cut into her. God, she'd done this to her son. "I'm sorry, Josh," she whispered. Tears stung her eyes. Turned him into a blur of distorted colour. She blinked, swiping at her face. "I never meant this...any of this. I was only..." She paused, bit her lips. "I was only thinking of you."

Josh turned back to her, slowly, his eyes red, his cheeks wet. "No, Mum. You were thinking of you."

"Josh." Nick's voice was low. Steady but cut with a strength Lauren didn't miss. "That's not fair. You don't know why she didn't tell you. But you're right about one thing. I *was* a prick, a selfish, thoughtless prick and because of that she did what she thought was the best for you."

Josh scrubbed a balled fist at his cheeks. He didn't look at any of them. "I've had enough of this shit," he muttered. "I'm outta here."

He pushed past them, shouldering his way between Lauren and Nick, eyes downcast, jaw muscles locked.

"Josh." Lauren turned, trying to snag his arm. Lord, how many times had she said his name? Was she incapable of saying anything else? So pathetic a mum she couldn't think of anything but her son's name to try to ease his pain? "Josh," she said again, hurrying after him.

But he didn't stop. She saw Aslin move, like a mountain moving toward the kitchen doorway. She saw Josh quicken his pace. The bodyguard's gaze flicked to her and then Josh burst into a sprint, running from the kitchen.

"Josh!" Lauren called, running after him.

Yeah, that's right, say his name one more time. That'll fix everything.

He didn't stop. The bang of the front door slamming shut was the only answer she got. Her feet stumbled, shock sinking like a pike into her brain, and she bit back a sob. Lord, how had this happened?

Every maternal instinct in her being told her to chase after him. To hold him. To take his pain and confusion away. Every other instinct—those of a person who'd experienced heartache—knew nothing would ease his pain at this very moment. Her son was angry with her, the angriest he'd ever been, and he had every right to be. She'd fucked up. Big time.

"I'll go after him, Miss R."

Lauren flinched. Rhys. She'd forgotten all about Rhys. She jerked her burning stare to her son's best friend, shame flooding through her. He hurried past, giving her a wry smile. The expression was at once totally uncharacteristic on the teenager's normally cheeky face and sympathetic beyond his young years. Fresh shame crashed over her, and then again when the front door banged like a shot over a silent battlefield.

Lauren let out a choked cry. Oh God, what had she done?

"He'll be okay." Nick's hand smoothed up her back. "He just needs some time."

Lauren closed her eyes. She sighed, her shoulders slumping. "I messed everything up." She shook her head, stepping away from him. His fingers slipped from her shoulder, trailing over her back as she twisted from his touch. "Everything."

"It wasn't exactly how I saw things going." His voice played over her nerves, so familiar, so soothing and yet so damn frustrating and confusing. "Do you want me to send Aslin after him?"

A lump sat in her throat, thick and heavy. She tried to swallow it away but it wouldn't go. Just like the guilt in her belly, it wouldn't go.

You should have told Josh. The second Nick turned up here in Murriundah, you should have told Josh who his father was. Instead, what did you do? Fuck. Fuck his father over and over again like a star-struck groupie.

She opened her eyes, studying the empty hallway stretching away from the kitchen. "No. I don't want anything from you, Nick."

"Lauren—" he reached for her but she shrugged his hand off her arm, "—don't be rash. Please, babe, don't be rash. Not after—"

"He's your son," she went on, ignoring the pressure on her chest, the numb emptiness in her heart, "and I can't keep you from seeing him, but *I* can't see you."

Nick's eyes narrowed. "Why? Because this is *my* fault?"

"No." She turned away from him, from the empty hallway stretching away to forever. "It's mine. All mine. I was too scared to tell Josh who his father was when he was old enough to know and I was too scared to tell him when you turned up at my house."

"But you don't have to be scared any more. He knows. What is there to be scared of?"

The lump in Lauren's throat grew thicker. "I'm scared of you, Nick. I'm scared of how much I love you, how much I need you. I'm defenseless against you and that scares the shit out of me. I'm a chicken, Nick. I know this. But I can't spend my life fighting the rest of the world for you." She snorted, a contemptuous little sound that tore at her soul. "I failed the first time I tried and never recovered."

Nick's jaw muscles knotted. He studied her, silent.

Take it back, Lauren. Take it all back. You can make it work this time. Take it back. Before you lose him again.

It was a beautiful fantasy. The kindergarten teacher and the rock star. A beautiful, wonderful, romantic fantasy. But it was just that—a fantasy.

She gave Nick a slow, sad smile. "You know the definition of insanity is doing the same thing over and over again and expecting a different result, right?"

He shook his head, his eyes never leaving her face. "I'd call it the definition of optimistic hope."

A laugh bubbled up Lauren's throat, fragile and soft and surprising. "You *are* a man of words, Nick. Powerful, soul-moving words. And it would be selfish of me to expect those words should only be for—"

A sharp, shrill ring made them both flinch. Nick bit back a growled curse. She crossed her kitchen to where her phone hung on the wall, a prickling tension sweeping over her. It would be Josh. Telling her he'd calmed down. Telling her she was a horrible mum. Telling her he didn't want anything to do with her again. Telling her he was—

She picked up the handset and put it to her ear. "Robbins' residence."

"I can't find him, Miss R," Rhys burst out. "I lost him in the dark and now I can't find him."

Ice-cold pressure crushed Lauren. Her face must have told Nick what was going on, that or he could hear Rhys's panic through the phone from where he stood. He turned to Aslin. "Go look. Find where he is, make sure he's okay and give me a call."

The massive man nodded, flicked Lauren an unreadable look and was gone. If she hadn't been so worried about Josh, she would have been impressed. But she was, and she couldn't be. Not at the moment.

"Miss Robbins?" Rhys's voice in her ear made her start. "Do you want me to come back? I've texted him but he's not answering."

She scrubbed her free hand over her eyes. How could she forget about her son's best friend again? Still on the other end of the phone line, still out in the cold?

God, you're a woeful piece of work, Lauren.

"Go home, Rhys," she instructed softly, letting him hear a calm she didn't feel. "It's too cold to be outside now." She slid her gaze to Nick where he stood watching her from the kitchen door, his face a study in controlled worry. "Josh'll calm down."

"If you're sure, Miss R." His teeth chattered through the response. "You know Josh. He's gotta blow off some steam a bit and then he'll be good. Nuthin' pisses him off for long. And I mean, Nick Blackthorne's his *dad*. The dude's gotta be freaking stoked about that."

Lauren felt her lips curl into a wry smile. "You're right, Rhys. And he probably will be once he forgives his mum for being a shit."

Rhys laughed. "You're not a shit, Miss R. Just really good at keepin' secrets."

The churning knot in her belly tightened. "Where are you? Need me to come get you? Take you home?"

"Nah, I can see the lights of my house from here. Tell Josh to text me when he gets home."

"Okay. Will you text me if he turns up at your house? Even if he doesn't want to talk to me, I'd like to know I can call off the dog squad."

Rhys laughed again at her desperate attempt at levity. "Shall do, Miss Robbins. Say goodnight to Nick for me. Tell him it was epic meeting him...err, right up to the last bit, that is."

Lauren chuckled, even though her belly was still twisting.

"Good night, Rhys. Send me a text me when you're home, okay? And tell your mum I'll call her tomorrow."

"I will. She heard Nick was in town. The barkeeper at the Cricketer's Arms has been telling everyone." The boy laughed again. "Wait until I tell her he's at your house. I bet she'll invite herself to breakfast."

Lauren closed her eyes again. That it was assumed Nick would still *be* at her house in the morning didn't surprise her. Talk travelled fast in a small town like Murriundah, even faster when it came to Nick Blackthorne. What surprised her was the fact that no one had guessed who Josh's father was before now.

It would have made things so much easier.

No, it wouldn't. Her not being a chicken, *that* would have made things easier. But she was. And now *here* she was, fucking up the lives of everyone she loved and cared for.

"Tell her I'll have the coffee brewing," she said into the phone, "but she's got to bring the croissants."

Rhys chuckled. "I'll keep texting Josh. Just in case, okay?"

"Okay. Night, Rhys."

She returned the phone to its cradle, a sigh slipping from her before she could stop it.

"He'll be okay." Nick stepped up behind her, smoothing his hands up her arms. "Aslin's out there looking for him. If the guy can find me a Vegemite sandwich in the middle of Yugoslavia he can find Josh."

Lauren knew he was trying to put her mind at rest. She knew that. And for a dizzying moment the urge to lean back into his strength, his warmth, flooded through her, so powerful she almost did. Almost. To feel his arms wrap around her, to feel his solid presence support her. God, how many times over the last fifteen years had she wished for that very thing? Too many times. Until she'd finally realized it was a stupid, empty

155

dream and gotten on with her life. Learned to lean on herself.

She walked away from him, out of the kitchen and into the living room, searching for her satchel. It was in here somewhere, and in it was her mobile. It made no sense, but her focus had become finding her phone. When she found her phone, she'd know what to do next.

Woeful, Lauren.

"Y'know, I know Murriundah like the back of my hand," Nick said from the entryway. "I could check all the places I used to go when I was pissed at Dad?"

Lauren couldn't stop her snorting chuckle. "If I remember correctly, those places were my old house, my tree house and the footbridge over Willows Creek, and I'm afraid to say all three have been demolished."

Nick turned his head, fist balling as he muttered something under his breath. He looked so much like his son at that point Lauren didn't know whether to laugh or cry. Instead, she returned her attention to finding her bag. She needed her phone. She'd send Josh a text. Tell him she was sorry. Ask him to come home so they could talk.

Ah, there it was. Right where she dumped it beside the sofa Friday night. God, was that only twenty-four hours ago? She crossed to her bag, the very bag given to her by the man whose gaze followed her now, snatched it from the floor and pulled her mobile from its innards.

Turning the device on, she blinked at the screen. Twenty-five text messages. Forty-two missed calls. How had she missed them?

Are you kidding? Life hasn't exactly been normal, has it? For Pete's sake, you were still in your PJs at two o'clock this afternoon.

"Lauren, we need to talk about this."

Ignoring him, she slid her thumb across her phone's screen and tapped on messages.

A string of them filled her screen, none of them from her son. All of them, save one, were about Nick.

Hey, Lauren, Gary White here. Your mechanic. I hear Nick Blackthorne's in town. Are U seeing him? Any chance U could get me his autograph?

Lauren, this is Milly Jenkins, Chris from soccer's mum. I was told you know Nick Blackthorne and that he's staying with you. Is that true? Night Whispers was my wedding song and I'd love to meet him. Would it be okay if we came around?

Hi, Lauren. The mayor would like to extend an invitation to you and Nick Blackthorne to attend dinner at his house Saturday evening. Please let me know by four o'clock Saturday. Thank you. Alysse Robertson.

They went on and on. All the same. All requests or hints or questions about Nick. Texts from people she rarely had anything more to do with than a smile if passing each other in the local market. Phone calls from numbers she didn't recognize. All of them. Except one text left on her phone at seven-forty five this morning from Jennifer.

Heya, gorgeous one. Hope you've calmed down after your sudden bolt from my home last night. I've been called to an emergency at Gonano's farm—one of his pregnant mares has gone down and the poor old bugger is beside himself. I'll call you when I get home. If you need me for anything at all, just give me a ring. Love you heaps. Jen. AKA wonder-vet and rock-star mender. PS, I know it's none of my business, but I think the guy is still seriously in love with you. You should have seen the gooey face he made when he was talking about you. Like, goo-ee. XXX

Hot tears prickled behind Lauren's eyes. Hot and so damn conflicted it was all she could do not to sob.

"Lauren." Nick's hands were cupping her jaw, lifting her face to him. "Babe, don't shut me out now. Not now." He brushed his thumb over her bottom lip. "Not ever."

She stared up into his eyes, eyes she knew so well. Eyes she saw every night in her dreams. Eyes she saw every time she looked at her son. "Will you hurt me again, Nick?"

The question left her on a whisper.

He smiled, a slow, cheeky smile that promised her the world. A smile she knew as well as his eyes. "No," he murmured. He lowered his head, touched his lips to hers.

And her mobile rang, the sound of Josh singing Bon Jovi's "Livin' on a Prayer" bellowing from her hand.

She stumbled back a step, blinking, her heart leaping like a petrified rabbit's. What the hell was she doing? Her son was somewhere out in the cold and she was kissing Nick? Kissing him? She snapped her stare to her phone, something akin to relief, something even closer to regret scorching through her at the image of a grinning Jennifer on her iPhone's screen.

She hit accept and pressed the phone to her ear. "Jen," she almost cried.

"You missing a family member, Miss Robbins?" her best friend asked. "'Cause I've got a cold, grumpy teenager sitting in my living room right at this very moment in time who insists he doesn't want to talk to his mum..." she paused, "*or* his dad for quite a while."

Chapter Eleven

Nick opened his eyes reluctantly, hissed sharply through his teeth and squeezed his eyes shut again. Fuck. Someone had opened the curtains through the night and the sun now streamed into his room like a golden bloody spotlight beam.

He pushed himself upright, squinting at the light. His head seemed to swim in a sickening spin, making his stomach lurch. He ground his teeth together, struggling with the nausea as he shifted on the bed and put his feet on the floor. "I feel like shit," he muttered, scratching at his hair.

"That's because you drank a bottle of scotch all by yourself last night," a husky female voice said to his right. "And apparently half a bottle of rum as well."

He opened his eyes and squinted some more at the petite woman dressed all in body-hugging red leather sitting cross-legged on the end of his bed. "What the fuck are you doing here, Frankie?"

His agent flashed a wide smile at him. "I heard my client was getting into a spot of bother in yonder sticks. Thought I better come and start negotiations with the locals as to who was going to pull you out of the river. I can't be forgetting my cut and all."

Nick let out a grunt, slumping back onto his bed. "I take it Aslin called you?"

"He did. And, thank bloody God, dressed you in your PJs before I got here as well, otherwise I'd be having nightmares. I'm a married woman, Nick Blackthorne. I don't need to find my clients sprawled out drunk in their hotel room beds at ten a.m. half naked. Well, I don't expect it from you anymore, that's for certain, although I have to say I like the black silk jammie dacks."

Nick scrunched up his face, his head throbbing. He tried to piece together the events of last night, but the only thing he could remember was Lauren telling him to leave. "I need some time away from you, Nick. I'm going to drive to Jennifer's, collect Josh and then bring him home and explain it all to him. I need to do that alone."

He'd argued of course, had damn near got down on his knees and begged, but she hadn't changed her mind. Nor had she answered her mobile when he'd called a few minutes after watching her drive away in her bombed-out old car.

I need some time away from you, Nick.

The words came back to him again, just as tormenting, as numbing as they'd been last night.

Some time away from you.

At some stage of the game, he must have walked back to the Cricketer's Arms. He must have bought a bottle of scotch and he must have drunk it. He didn't remember. He didn't remember Aslin finding him either, but that must have happened as well. He especially didn't remember buying a bottle of rum. He hated rum, but obviously his mood last night hadn't. So for the second night in a row, he'd ended up drunk in his hometown's only pub. The prodigal son returns. And to think he hadn't touched a drop of alcohol for close to two years.

"She doesn't want me, Frankie."

The words left him on a breathless moan. He raised the

heel of his palms to his eyes and pushed. Pain rolled through his head, cold and aching and real. He could grasp this pain. It made sense. But the pain in his heart... Jesus, he couldn't comprehend it. How could he, when Lauren had never caused him pain before?

"She doesn't want me," he repeated.

He felt the mattress shift and then Frankie was sitting beside him. "And what does this mean, exactly?"

The question was soft. Curious.

"It means..." He swallowed, his throat as scratchy and dry as shit. "It means once again, I'm denied my family."

"So, are you thinking of you in this situation or Lauren and your son?"

He opened his eyes and studied her through a hazy blur. "Did Aslin tell you?"

She nodded. "But only after I read about it in the *Sydney Morning Herald*'s front page this morning on the drive up." She shifted a little on the bed, crossing her leather-clad ankles and hooking her elbows around her knees. "By the way, you owe Alec breakfast in bed. It was my turn to cook and instead we drove up here. I really can't believe you grew up in such a tiny town."

"You made your husband drive to Murriundah?" Nick scrubbed at his face. "Man, he must really love you."

Frankie grinned at him. "He does, thank you very much. And that's what love is—putting the other person first. Now tell me, what are you putting Lauren ahead of? What are you putting your son ahead of?"

Nick dropped his hands from his face. He rolled his head, squinting up at his agent. "I told her I loved her. I told her I would quit music for her. For them both."

Frankie raised her eyebrows. "Well, shit, that's not the kind of thing you're meant to tell your agent, hon."

He chuckled, a weak, mirthless laugh that barely left his chest. "'S'true though. And even that wasn't enough."

"Make it enough."

Frankie's flat statement jerked his stare to her face. She was studying him, brilliant sharp blue eyes intent.

"Now here's the thing, Nick Blackthorne," she went on. "I make squillions off you every year. Enough to retire and get fat on the residues. But I'm also your friend. And I know how downright bloody miserable you've been since...well, since almost ever. The Nick I know is not the Nick I know is in there. That Nick, *that's* the Nick I saw singing "Gotta Run" sixteen-and-a-half years ago to a girl in the audience at the Sydney Opera House, a girl with wild strawberry blonde hair and freckles to die for. *That* Nick, he fucking well burned with passion and life and love."

Nick's stomach rolled. He remembered that concert. A charity event for Kids with Cancer. He remembered it because it was the last time Lauren had come to any of his concerts after being almost attacked during the event by a horde of women standing around her when he'd sung. She'd needed escorting from the crowd by the hired muscle. He'd been worried sick until he saw her again. Sixteen-and-a-half years ago. How things had changed. Now she'd just slam them all with her satchel.

A warm pride flowed through him as he pictured this new Lauren he'd come to know in the last few days dealing with maniacal groupies. There'd be no contest. She'd eat them alive and leave their bones for the birds to pick at.

He frowned, resting himself on his elbows. Something about Frankie's tale itched at the back of his head. "How old are you, Frankie?"

She grinned. "None of your fucking business, Blackthorne. Old enough to be at that concert, is all you need to know. Old enough to see footage of you at that concert on Dad's VCR." She pulled a melodramatic face. "VCR? Wow, you old guys had some clunky shit technology back in the Stone Ages."

"Did you come all this way to insult me?"

She grinned again. "No. I came to make sure you're okay. To see if what Aslin says is true. And even lying here in this hotel-room bed, wearing a three-day growth and desperately in need of some toothpaste or mouthwash, I can see it is. That fire is in you again. Lauren Robbins, school teacher extraordinaire, makes you burn like no other, Nicky-boy."

The observation set a flutter going in the pit of Nick's belly. Frankie, and Aslin it seemed, was right. So damn right. He raked his nails across his scalp. "So what do I do about it? Go bang down her door, sweep her up onto my horse and take her away? Stopping only to grab my son?"

Frankie cocked an eyebrow. "You could, but that would likely only piss her off."

Nick snorted. "Yeah. You could say that. And at this point, I don't know if Josh wants anything to do with me."

"But you want to be in his life?"

Her question, asked with a deceptive calm, made him narrow his eyes. "Of course I do. Jesus, Frankie, do you really think I'd be in this state if I didn't?"

"The thing is," she went on, her expression...guarded. "I know what it's like to have a celebrity father. What it's like to grow up in a celebrity's world. It fucks with your head, Nick. Big time. You're not the average father material, I have to point out here, and Josh is already getting a taste of it. He's been named in the media, his photograph is on the front page of the country's biggest newspaper, his school records are probably being dredged up from any source the muck-gathering gossip reporters can find, his Facebook account hacked, his friends already interrogated over the phone and in person, and it's only ten a.m.. That's not going to stop any time soon. And every time you're photographed with someone not Lauren, hell, it could be me for all it matters, Josh will be reading headlines the next day about his father having an affair. You know that, right? Are you ready to thrust him into that? To throw him into that life? Knowing what it's like? Knowing what it can do to you?"

Nick's heart leapt into his throat. He pictured Josh, the kid who turned bright red when asking about groupies. He thought of his son, smiling like a little boy at Christmas when asked if he wanted to go on a helicopter. He pictured him being harassed by reporters and gossip-rag journoes, mics in his face, camera flashes popping in his eyes...

The blood drained from Nick's face. He sat upright, grabbing Frankie by the arms. "What did you say? Something about his friends being interrogated in person and it's only ten a.m.?" Frankie nodded. "They're here? The press? They're here and they're seeking out Josh's friends? Already?"

She nodded again. "I overheard one of them complain down in the foyer that some kid called Rhys told him to, and I quote, stick his camera up his arse and take a photo of his shit. I have to admit, I think I like this Rhys kid already."

Rhys's response should have made Nick chuckle. But he couldn't. His life, his rock-star life had invaded his son's. Everything Lauren knew and feared.

"Have they got to Lauren?" He swallowed, his mouth like dust. "To Josh?"

Frankie shook her head. "They're camped out at her home. The whole bloody Sydney horde as far as I can tell, but that mountain you call a bodyguard is keeping them at bay. It won't be long though before even his mammoth menace doesn't scare them enough. Once they get the scent—a glimpse of Lauren or your son through a crack in the curtains perhaps—they'll swarm like the ghouls they are." Her expression turned dark, angry. "You know what they're like, Nick. You've been dealing with them for almost seventeen years."

Nick's gut rolled. He had. And it was brutal. He shot to his feet, dragging his hands through his hair. Fuck, where were his clothes? Where the fuck were his clothes? He had to get out there. He had to get to Lauren, to Josh. He had to show his son how to deal with—

"You know if you go there now you'll only stir up more shit for them?"

He froze on Frankie's low statement.

"You arrive at her house and they'll never leave her alone. And you've lost her. Lost them both, maybe."

He dropped back onto the edge of the bed, cold emptiness settling in his stomach. Frankie was right. He did know that. The first few weeks of being hounded by the press had been a massive ego boost for twenty-year-old Nick Blackthorne, the next few months, a pain in the arse, the next sixteen years, hell. And he'd been expecting it. Josh, however...Lauren...

He thought of the woman he loved. Thought of everything she'd lost due to his fame. The future she thought she was going to have when she'd up and moved from the safety of her small-town home to the big concrete jungle that was Sydney with him at the ripe old age of eighteen, the happy-ever-after he'd promised her when they were just innocent teenagers in love. And now she was losing the future she'd made for herself. Even with him not in her life, hers was being fucked over.

A noise rumbled low in his chest, a growl of angry contempt. "I can't do nothing, Frankie."

Her lips curled, the smile of an agent with a reputation for being ruthless. Married life may have brought out the romantic in her, but Frankie Winchester was still an agent. A bloody brilliant one. "Call a press announcement. Call a press announcement to be held outside this very pub. It'll put it on the map and make the proprietor a fortune—Cricketer's Arms, the place Nick Blackthorne announced his retirement after his one and only show on the Tropical Sin Tour in Sydney."

He blinked. He hadn't seen that coming.

Frankie chuckled. "It's what you want, isn't it? Lauren, Josh? A life with them, not on the road? A normal life doing normal things with normal people?"

"Yeah, *hell* yeah, but I didn't expect my *agent* to tell me to do it."

She shrugged, flipping a fat, round curl from in front of her eyes as she did so. "I've made gazillions out of you, Nicky-boy. And I'll make even more whether you keep singing or not. Besides, I married a millionaire gardener with clients richer than us both. I'm not worried about where my next meal comes from." She slid her hands over her belly, a slow caress Nick couldn't miss. "Or my family's, for that matter."

He jerked his stare to her face, down to her belly, noticing for the first time the small but pronounced swell under the snug leather of her biker vest. "Are you...?"

She grinned once again, a smile so stunning, so happy Nick forgot to breathe for a second.

"It's a brave new world, Nick Blackthorne. You've just got to grab it."

He was on his feet again, prowling the room for his clothes. Grab it? He was going to strangle the bloody thing. Lauren had asked for him to give her time? He would give her time. Time to buy a paper. Time to turn on a radio. Time to read her damn

Twitter feed if she had one. Just time to discover what he was about to announce to the world. Time to learn he was serious about her, about Josh, about them.

He snatched up his jeans, decidedly worse for wear after last night, but he couldn't be bothered getting a clean pair out of his bag. It didn't matter what he was wearing, only what he said. Not the music, just the words.

"Go call a press conference, agent of mine." He threw Frankie a quick look as he shook out his crumpled jeans. "I'll be down in thirty minutes. And get Aslin on the phone. I want him as close to Lauren and Josh as she'll let him."

Frankie snapped off a salute. *"Jawohl, herr kommandant."*

He gave her a wide smirk. "Oh, and Mrs. Harris? I'm stripping out of these PJs now so if you don't want to see..."

She was out of his room quick smart, designer biker boots thumping on the floor, a loud and thoroughly melodramatic, "ewww," following her flee.

With a snort and a shake of his head, Nick shoved his pyjama trousers down over his hips. The black silk pooled at his feet and he kicked the garment aside and shoved his legs in his jeans without bothering with boxers. He tugged up the zip, buttoned the fly and it hit him. A simple sentence on a simple rhythm.

I'll hold you till you let me.

He straightened, the line whispering through his head again, but this time, there were more. So many more. Words on a rhythm. Words he couldn't ignore. He ran to his overnight bag, dug around in its contents, the words not just whispering to him now, but singing. Singing.

I'll hold you till you let me.

And then plead for time...

"Yes!" he shouted, finding what he was looking for. A pen.

His notebook.

He spun to the bed, dropped to his knees and opened the book, uncaring that it wasn't to the newest clean page. It didn't matter. The words, he needed to get the words down.

I'll hold you till you let me.

And then plead for time

To let you know I'm sorry

To make you mine.

I never should have left you

Never should have caused you pain.

But in the hearts of fools and men

Love will come undone again.

I can't promise no tears

But I promise utter truth

And in that truth I'll show you how

I'll hold you for all time.

My heart, I give you mine today

Today.

My heart, I give you mine today

Today.

The words flowed from him, coming so fast his hand could barely form them. He scratched out notes, indicated inflections, pace, but it was the words that made him burn. The words that spoke of his soul.

They kept coming. Verse followed by chorus. Chorus followed by bridge. Bridge followed by verse and back to bridge again.

Words that promised. Words that sang.

An outpouring beyond constraint.

He saw the music and heard the words, writing it all down,

notes and rests marked on a hastily drawn staff, key signatures indicated, time signature likewise. A song called "Today".

He was still writing, his knees beyond numb, his hand beginning to cramp, when the door to his room opened and Aslin stepped across the threshold.

Nick's heart leapt into his throat. If Aslin was here, that could only mean Lauren and Josh were as well. His bodyguard wouldn't leave them to the mercy of the paparazzi. His heart hammering faster, he stared at the man, waiting to see Lauren step from behind Aslin's menacing frame. Waited to hear his son's voice—deep with looming adulthood and yet still the voice of youth.

Holding Nick's stare, Aslin closed the door behind him.

Nick frowned. "What are you doing, As? Where's Lauren? Josh?"

The ex-SAS commando shook his head. "Sorry, Nick."

"What do you mean, sorry?" He threw the pen on the bed and pushed himself to his feet. His knees, bent for so long on the hard wooden floor they screamed at him. Blood rushed back into his calves, his toes, like a million fire ants biting into his flesh. He gave Aslin a puzzled look. "You didn't leave them there alone, did you?"

Aslin shook his head again, his expression...bleak.

Jesus, why was Aslin's expression so bleak?

He swallowed, the pit of his gut heavy. "Where's Lauren, As? Where's Josh? Is he okay?" A thought struck him, cold and terrible. "Did he come home last night? Shit, I have no fucking clue. So fucking deep in a bottle I have no clue. Is he okay? Is that why—"

"He came home, Nick," Aslin spoke over him, his voice more like thunder than ever. "He's fine. They're both fine. After I got you into bed last night I went back there and kept an eye on the place."

Nick felt his frown deepen. "So why are you here now?"

Aslin studied him for a long moment, as if he wasn't sure how to answer the question. Finally, with a muttered curse and a shake of his head, he looked at Nick and said, "They've gone."

Nick blinked. "Who? The paparazzi?"

"Lauren and Josh."

The two names hit Nick like a double blow from a fist. "What do you mean, gone?"

"Fifteen minutes ago, Lauren and Josh climbed into her car with two overnight bags and left. She almost ran down one idiot who thought he'd take a photo from the middle of her driveway."

The heavy weight in his gut grew cold. Tight. He dragged his hands through his hair, his gaze going to the notepad opened upon his bed. To the music, the lyrics written there. Overnight bags. Jesus, she'd left with overnight bags.

He turned back to Aslin. "Where were they going?"

His bodyguard let out a sigh, the unsteady sound utterly alien from him. "I don't know. She wouldn't tell me. I followed her out of town though, long enough to be satisfied none of the pap were following. She drives fast, Nick. Wherever she's going, she isn't being followed by the scum with cameras." He pulled a folded piece of paper from his back pocket and handed it to Nick, that same bleak expression falling over his face again. "She gave me this and asked if I'd give it to you."

Nick swallowed, taking the offered note. He opened the folded paper, reading the three words written on it.

Three words.

Like a curse.

He looked up from the message, his throat thick. "Did she

take her satchel?"

For the fourth time, Aslin shook his head.

It was the fourth shake that told Nick what he didn't want to know. Lauren had left her satchel behind. He knew the significance of that. Knew what Lauren was saying to him through it. Last night she'd told him she was scared of him, how she felt for him. Today she was telling him he was like a curse. And right now, as he stood here in the *penthouse* room of The Cricketer's Arms, with the country's media no doubt swarming outside, awaiting a press conference where he would announce he was quitting the biz for her, she was driving out of Murriundah. Driving away from him.

Taking his son with her. His family gone from his life. Again.

Closing his eyes, Nick dropped onto the edge of the bed, hung his head between his knees, crumpled Lauren's note in his fist and cried.

Chapter Twelve

Eight days had passed. Eight days of confused pain, wretched doubt, raw truth and solitary tears. Eight days camped out in a two-bedroom holiday apartment in a coastal town almost as small as Murriundah seven hours north. Eight days spent walking the chilly winter beach alone, thinking about it all. Eight days talking with Josh, apologizing for her stupid behaviour. Eight days listening to every song Nick Blackthorne had ever recorded over and over again.

Eight days reading the national papers, the gossip magazines. Eight days of seeing her own face in them, seeing the image of her standing in her open front door, dressed only in her pyjama shirt, her hair a mess, a half-dressed Nick behind her, his hair equally so. Of seeing Josh on those pages, his image inevitably superimposed next to ones of his father—her son looking stunned and nervous, Nick always looking sexy and confident and every inch the rock star he was.

Eight days of speculation about her history with Nick, interviews with people she barely knew who called themselves her close friends and trusted sources, people who spilled facts so ridiculous she would have laughed if she wasn't so pissed off. Facts about her so-called obsession with Nick, how she stalked him, blackmailed him. Facts about Josh's so-called developmentally delayed abilities, about Nick's shame that his son was impaired and that's why he'd been hidden from the world. Facts that stated Josh was a musical idiot savant who mimicked Nick pitch-perfect. Facts that were nothing more than fabricated bullshit, written to feed the masses hungry for gossip on Nick Blackthorne.

None of the papers and magazines, it seemed, had any real clue where Nick was during her eight days in hiding either. There'd been no statement from him, no response to the articles revealing Josh and Lauren. The only hint someone had talked to him was a press release from Walter Winchester, Nick's record producer, who announced Nick's latest album, simply titled "Blackthorne", would be releasing in two weeks time. There was an image of the man beside an enlarged version of the cover, an image of Nick taken who knows when holding up a hand as if fighting off unwanted media attention.

Lauren didn't know how he lived with it. By the end of the eight days, she was ready to scream. Josh however, had taken a different route.

He'd stubbornly refused to talk to her for two days, had done little except text Rhys on that first day, telling him his mum had "lost her freaking mind". He'd shown her the text, eyes flat, glare angry, just before hitting send. Whatever Rhys had texted back had made him angrier, and he'd shoved his phone in his pocket and ignored it for the remainder of the day. At the end of the second day of silence, he'd found an article in the *Sydney Morning Herald* that went on at length about Nick and Lauren's life before Nick became famous. Lauren had found him regarding her with a contemplative stare more than once. By the middle of the third day, and after numerous text conversations with God knows who, he'd flopped onto the sofa beside her and given her a relaxed hug. "I freaked out a bit back at home, didn't I?"

She'd shaken her head, letting him see her understanding

smile. "You had reason."

He'd chuckled, the sound so like his father Lauren had caught her bottom lip with her teeth. "Guess I take after you when it comes to the dramatics, 'eh?"

Lauren had rolled her eyes. "And you don't think your dad's got any talent for putting on a show when he needs to?"

The words were meant to be cutting. She was still angry, damn it. The trouble was they didn't sound angry at all. They sounded...sad.

Josh's smile had turned lop-sided, another Nick trait. "I think I'd like to learn all sorts of things about my dad that the rest of the world hasn't read in a magazine, or watched on MTV."

He'd dropped a quick kiss on her cheek then, and scrambled out of the sofa before she could do anything stupid like cry and try to kiss him in return. He knew her well. He was her son, after all.

"Josh," she'd said, and maybe it was the hesitancy in her voice that made him stop, turn back to her and grin.

"I read an article today in one of the papers," he said, the lop-sided smile stretching a little wider, "that discusses my apparent ability to attract members of the opposite sex at ease already. It seems that, even at such a young age, my 'burgeoning good looks and soulful voice' are the stuff of teenage girls' fantasies. Apparently, I'm going to get lucky a lot."

She'd crossed her arms and given him an exasperated look. "Your point being, Joshua William Robbins?"

He'd shrugged. "It's good to know where all these 'burgeoning' good looks come from, I guess. Who I need to thank. Not some faceless guy who may have been a fuckwit."

Lauren had groaned at his language. "Josh."

"Sorry, Mum." He'd frowned then, his hands sliding into the back pockets of his jeans, his eyes intent. "*Is* Nick a fuckwit? Is that why we're here, hiding out?"

The sigh left her before she could stop it. A serious case of the knots twisted in her stomach. "No, Josh. Your father is not a...not a fuckwit."

His frown had deepened. "So why are we here, then? 'Cause it seems to me the best reason for having Nick Blackthorne as my dad is because he's a nice guy who makes you laugh and smile like I've never seen you do before."

Lauren's heart had smashed into her throat. She'd stared at him, unable to think of a thing to say.

After that, it had just been her on a solo quest for resolution. Josh seemed to know exactly what he wanted—to get to know his dad better—and spent the days fishing on the beach and making a scrapbook of cuttings about his infamy and his infamous parents, suggesting regularly she was being a bit of a drama queen and really should at least call Nick. She'd told him so often he was too young to understand that the words made little sense. But then again, perhaps they never really had. Josh had found his father. His father had made him laugh and grin and promised to keep him safe. What else was there to understand?

And so it was that on the eighth day she packed them both up and drove home. She still had no bloody clue what she was going to do about the whole Nick situation, but life had to go on. She'd taken a week off work she couldn't really afford. KR needed her. Awaited her return.

If she was lucky, Murriundah had moved on and she could slip back into her normal life with just a smile and a, "you know, it was one of those things" to pass off the whole thing.

Jennifer had other plans.

Her best friend was waiting for her when she arrived home early Sunday night, a grin on her face, a bottle of champagne in her hand.

"Heya, Jen," Josh called, climbing out of the passenger seat of Lauren's car before she could even engage the handbrake. "What are we celebrating?"

"We are celebrating your mum being the most famous person I know."

Lauren rolled her eyes, slamming her car door shut behind her. The icy winter night wrapped around her. "I'm pretty certain you know someone more famous than me, Jen."

Jennifer smacked her forehead, her breath white clouds puffing from her lips. "You're right. I know Josh."

Josh laughed. "Sign you an autograph for fifty bucks."

Jennifer's eyebrows shot up with exaggerated shock. "Fifty bucks?"

He shrugged. "I want to buy a guitar."

"Why don't you just borrow one of your dad's?"

Lauren gave her best friend a flat glare.

"Because *she*—" Josh tossed his head in Lauren's direction, "—hasn't decided if we're talking to him or not."

Jennifer rolled her eyes this time, walked down the front porch steps, kissed Lauren on the cheek and then handed her the bottle of champagne. "Well, Josh, I think it's time I save you from your dithering old mum and take you somewhere fun. Oh, did you hear that? I'm a poet and didn't know it."

Josh groaned. "That's lame, Jen."

She grinned. "That it is, sorry. Anyways, grab your bag from your mum's car. I'm dropping you at Rhys's for some teenage therapy after your week of maternal suffocation. Mrs. McDowell has your bed made up, as far as I know there's a bowl of spaghetti bolognaise waiting for you and I've already got your school clothes and stuff in my truck."

"Serious?" Josh turned to Lauren with a hopeful look. "Can I go, Mum? Please?"

Lauren noted his excitement, his fidgeting anticipation. Eight days was a long time to go without a best mate at fifteen. An even longer time when you were stuck with just your unhinged mother for company and no Wii or Playstation to escape to. She chuckled, nodding her head. He needed to be away from her for a bit. She understood that. He may not have completely forgiven her for the secret she'd kept from him, but he'd moved on. Wasn't it time she did that same?

In what way? Even if the world has found something else far more interesting than you, even if Nick has given up his foolish notion of the fantasy happy-ever-after and gone back to the life of a rock star, do you really think you'll be able to move on? Do you?

The question was the most vexing and one she'd yet to find an answer to. But that shouldn't stop her son getting on with his life. Whether his father was in it or not.

With a grin, Josh gave her another one of his rare hugs. "Love you, Mum," he whispered. "You are the best, you know that? A bit messed up, but still the best."

He bounded away before she could crush him in a bear hug. Without any sign of remorse or despair for deserting his mother in favour of his best friend, he pulled his overnight bag from the back of Lauren's car and hurried to Jennifer's pickup.

Lauren watched him, a sigh welling in her chest. Tears prickled at the back of her eyes. Happy tears.

"Ah, the resilience of youth." Jen chuckled. She slipped her arm around Lauren's waist and gave her a gentle squeeze. "Doesn't it make you sick?"

"Thanks, Jen." Lauren nudged her friend's hip with hers. "He needed this."

Jennifer fixed her with a sideward gaze. "You need it too." She tapped the bottle of champagne in Lauren's hand. "And this. A glass or two to celebrate coming through the most amazing...shit without losing your mind."

Lauren pulled a face. "Didn't I? I have to admit, my mind feels kinda unhinged at the moment."

Jennifer pulled a face back, equally dismissive. "No, you didn't. You wouldn't be standing here if you had, letting your son spend a night at his best friend's." She dropped a kiss on Lauren's cheek and gave her another squeeze. "Now get yourself inside, teach. You've got school tomorrow and a room full of six-year-olds who haven't seen their famous teacher for a whole week. Besides, I don't know about you, but I'm freezing my arse off out here."

Two minutes later, Lauren climbed the steps of her front porch, the sound of Jennifer's pickup rumbling down the road fading behind her. Opening her door, she was greeted with the smell of freshly brewed coffee and the crackling whispers of a fire. She smiled, entering her toasty-warm home. She had to give it to Jennifer she really knew how to look after dumb animals like her.

Stripping off her jacket and scarf, she made her way into the living room, dropped onto her old sofa and toed off her boots. An ice bucket sat on the coffee table, along with two glasses from Lauren's rather forlorn crystal collection.

Lauren cocked an eyebrow at them. Okay, so Jen was brilliant with dumb animals but she couldn't count for shit.

A glass of champagne later, Lauren settled back into her sofa, crossed her ankles beside the remaining glass and closed her eyes. And heard the singing. A male voice the entire world knew singing words she didn't know, accompanied by the simple strings of an acoustic guitar.

Her heart thumped its way into her throat. Hard. Fast. Her eyes snapped open.

Nick.

Nick Blackthorne was outside her door. Singing.

"...make you mine.

I never should..."

Lauren caught her bottom lip with her teeth, the soft, barely heard words playing over her senses. Making her breath quicken, her palms tingle and the pit of her belly flip.

"In the hearts of fools and men

Love will come undone again."

He was here. On the other side of her door, singing about love and regret and mistakes. Singing about them.

Oh, Lord. Did she really want to open the door?

Of course you do.

He stopped playing the second she did. Stood staring at her through the artful mess of his black hair, his jaw darkened with a shadow well past five o'clock, his tall, lean body dressed in black, his guitar—the one his mum had given him for his eighteenth birthday—hanging from his shoulder on a wide band, the very band Lauren had given him as a present for the same birthday. The epitome of a rock star.

She gazed at him. Ate him up with her eyes. And knew, there and then, she could never be what he needed. He was song and she was roll call.

He was a gift to the world. She was on playground duty.

She opened her lips, ready to tell him, accepting the truth as much as she hated that it was so. She loved him, Lord, she loved him. And because she loved him she couldn't be with him.

He was music and she was small-town and that was the way it would always be.

She opened her lips and he stepped across the threshold and kissed her.

His lips made love to hers. There was no other way to describe the kiss. It wasn't fierce and it wasn't dominating. It wasn't urgent or hungry or desperate. It was love. It was passion in its purest form. He kissed her, only his lips touching her. Only his lips. The cold night air from outside swirled around her ankles, her legs, and she burned anyway, Nick's kiss setting her on fire. A kiss unlike any he'd ever given her before.

He kissed her and when she stepped back into her house, he moved with her, his lips still making love to hers. He kissed her and when she whimpered into his mouth, he closed the door behind him with his foot and kissed her some more.

He kissed her, just kissed her, until her head spun and her knees trembled and she could barely think who she was.

And somewhere between her front door and her living room, he stopped his kiss long enough to remove his guitar, but Lauren didn't know when. Somewhere between the front door and her sofa, he stopped his kiss long enough to strip her of her clothes, to strip himself of his clothes. Long enough to bury his face between her thighs, to use his tongue to bring her to an orgasm so powerful she felt sure the whole world heard, and then he was kissing her again. Then his lips were making love to hers again and music and playground duty were the furthest thing from her mind.

He slid inside her, his body moving over hers as she lay stretched out on her sofa, his kiss worshipping her mouth, his length embedded deep in her heat. He slid inside her, moved inside her, and there were no words. There were no words, no music, nothing but the rhythm of their hearts beating, the moans of their pleasure, the sound of their lovemaking. It was the most haunting, beautiful song Lauren had ever heard.

And it was enough. It was all she needed. For now, it was all she needed.

They climaxed together, both silent. Nick tore his lips from hers, gazing into her eyes as their releases shuddered through them, his nostrils flaring, his forehead slicked with perspiration. They came together and before her climax left her, he withdrew from her sex and brought her to climax again with his lips and tongue and teeth. Again and again. Never saying a word.

He drew one orgasm after another from her until he was hard once more. So hard, and then he thrust back inside her, filling her, completing her, and they began the exquisite, rapturous journey to release together all over again.

Time ceased to exist. All there was for Lauren was Nick and the pleasure he gave her. Pleasure so raw and elemental even if she wanted to tell him this was their last night, their last moment, words failed her. At some point, they moved to her bedroom, but she didn't know when. Only when the soft kiss of her duvet on her flush skin told her so, did she realize where they were. How many orgasms after the living room? She didn't know. Didn't care.

They made love to each other over and over again, their pleasure keeping them warm, their bodies twin entities of molten desire fuelling each other. They made love and they kissed and sometimes they just held each other and that was as perfect and powerful and right as everything else. And finally, when there was no more strength in their bodies, Nick tucked her into the curve of his body, laying his arm over her waist, his long thighs pressing to the backs of hers, his lips pressed to the back of her head.

"Nick," she began. She had to tell him this was goodbye. She had to. It tore her apart to do so, but she had to.

"Shh, babe," he murmured, tugging her closer to his body. "No words tonight, okay? There'll be time for words tomorrow, but not now. Let it just be this now. Just us. Please, Lauren?"

The request made her throat tight. She closed her eyes and smoothed her hand over his arm, finding his fingers and threading hers through them. "Just this," she whispered, even as her heart ached.

When she woke the next morning, but a few hours later, he was gone, a small note left on the pillow where his head had lain. *Have a performance to prepare for. N.*

She stared at the note, at the six simple words that spoke the truth louder than any either of them had uttered since Nick had returned to Murriundah. She bit back a choked sob. He'd chosen his music over her, as she knew he eventually would. As she knew he should. Damn it, why was she so upset? This was what she wanted, wasn't it? This was what she knew had to be.

But it wasn't. Somewhere during the night, somewhere between the first moment she'd heard him singing on her front porch and the last moment she'd heard him whisper her name, she'd let herself believe their fantasy could come true.

Because she was an idiot.

Climbing out of bed, she hurried to the shower. The pipes groaned, protesting the chill strangling them, refusing to give her anything more than a tepid stream of water. "Welcome back to reality, Lauren." She dashed from the bathroom, refusing to look at her clock as she dressed for school. She knew what it would tell her—that she was late—but it wasn't that which caused her to keep her gaze from the time device on her bedside table. It was the simple fact there was no way she could look at the clock and not see her bed. Her bed and the tousled sheets and the indent on the pillow where Nick's head had been.

She let out a growl, shoved her feet into a pair of black knee high boots and ran from her room. If she was really lucky the gods of idiotic females would come into her house while she was at school and take her bed away, replacing it with a nice new one, preferably single and not smelling of Nick.

Her students were waiting for her when she walked into her room five minutes after the bell for class chimed. They watched her enter the room from their desks, silent, their eyes wide, their stares following her as she crossed to her desk and deposited her satchel beside her chair. A giggle slipped from someone, followed by someone else going, "shush". Lauren felt her cheeks turn red.

Great. She was embarrassed by a kindergartener. Brilliant. Bloody brilliant.

Turning to her class, she gave them all a big, cheery smile. "Good morning, KR."

"Good morning, Miss Robbins," they chorused back. Someone giggled again.

"Did you miss me?" she asked, perching herself on the edge of her desk and casting them all a slow inspection before pulling a wounded-puppy expression. "Or did you have so much fun with Ms. Affleck you didn't want me to come back?"

"We missed you, Miss Robbins," Thomas Missen called out.

She smiled, affecting a relieved sigh. "Ah, that's good. I missed you too. Now, who can tell me what we are going to—"

A long bell cut her short, followed by another. The Special Assembly bell.

Lauren frowned, straightening from her desk. "What's going on?" she asked her class as she crossed to her room's door. There wasn't a special assembly scheduled for today, not that she knew of. She turned back to KR, more than a little surprised to find them all standing in a nice, neat row behind her, their faces fighting wide grins to stay serious.

She raised her eyebrows, and then started when a loud whoop shattered the quiet playground beyond her door and Mr. Kransky's Year Six class went running, in their normal helter-skelter way, past her room toward the assembly area.

Lauren turned back to her class and shrugged. "Okay," she said. "Looks like something fun is happening."

She led her students out the door and along the walkway, more than impressed with how straight and controlled they were. Rarely did they walk to assembly with such determined poise. Rachel Jones slid her gaze to Lauren, a giggle bubbling past her lips before Thomas Missen gave her a nudge with his elbow, a glowering glare and another fierce, "*shhh*".

Lauren narrowed her eyes. Something was going on. Something...

The thought didn't finish forming in Lauren's mind. It faded away to be replaced by stunned confusion. The assembly area was packed with people. Not just school people, not just students and teachers, but parents and members of the Murriundah population as well. Standing around the edges of the area as the other classes marched into their assigned places, chatting to each other, waving to their children, some taking photos.

Lauren frowned. What the hell was going on?

She jerked her attention from the unexpected sight back to her own class, and blinked.

KR weren't sitting on the two straight purple lines that indicated their place for assembly. KR were organizing themselves on the assembly stage at the front of the school, standing in neat rows, tallest students at the back, their faces no longer serious but beaming. Beaming.

They all looked at her, and with a quick glance to someone Lauren couldn't see, Thomas Missen stepped forward, his cheeks growing bright red, his spine growing straighter.

"Good morning, teachers, students and guests to Murriundah Public School." His young voice rose above the noise of the crowd, trembling with nerves. Everyone fell silent. Everyone. An event Lauren had never, ever experienced in her entire twelve-and-a-half years of teaching. "Today, we, Miss Robbins's kindergarten class, would like to present to you a special musical performance conducted by a special guest who was once a student of our school."

Lauren's lips began to tingle. The hair on the back of her neck stood on end. Her breath grew quick and her stomach flip-flopped.

The note Nick had left for her on his pillow came back to her, six words she thought spoke the truth. *Have a performance to prepare for.*

She blinked, suddenly aware every stare in the assembly area was on her. Every stare, including Jennifer's and Josh's, who seemed to materialize out of the crowd, Jennifer's smile devilish, Josh's goofy. And so very, very impressed.

She blinked, her heart slamming harder into her throat.

And then Nick walked up onto the stage. Nick, dressed in old jeans, a green and gold Australian Rugby Union jersey and a red and blue Murriundah Public School scarf.

Nick.

Lauren's mouth went dry.

He found her stare with his, gave her a smile, gave the audience another one and then turned to KR and nodded to Thomas.

The little boy all but quivered. "For Miss Robbins," he said loudly, a beat before twenty-two six-year-olds began singing

185

"Whispers in the Night", their collective voices rising up with beautiful, child-like harmony. Singing to Lauren the words she knew were forever written on her soul.

"This life of mine is empty
Since I walked away
Taking paths I haven't seen
Looking for roads I've left behind
Searching for an answer
That was always there
Needing to feel something
Beyond this pain.

And I want to beg but I can't find the words
And I want to cry but I can't find the tears
And all that's left is the shadow of your heart and the ghost of your smile
And the whispers in the night."

The song continued, words of tormented broken dreams and longing for something lost until the last line faded away. Until the children's voices grew softer, softer and they finished singing.

Their stares stayed glued to Nick's face, their expressions so earnest and serious as the last word left them all in nothing but a collected sigh, and then all twenty-two student were looking at her.

Looking at her with joy and hope so innocent that she wanted to cry.

No, that wasn't why she wanted to cry. She wanted to cry because Nick was standing before her school, her class, the whole world, watching her from across the other side of the assembly area, his smile nervous, nervous goddamn him. She wanted to cry because everyone was clapping and cheering and looking at her, and her class was beaming and she'd never felt so special. So special and loved and...and...damn it, so Nick's.

She stared at him across the heads of the student body, her heart in her throat.

Oh Lord, what did she do now?

Her lips curled into a slow smile, a second before she realized the assembly area was silent again. Silent. As if waiting.

A silence broken again by Thomas Missen's loud, clear voice. "As Mr. Blackthorne's representative I would like to take this opportunity to announce that he is retiring from singing professionally." The crowd gasped, a shocked ripple rolling over everyone. Everyone that was, except Nick and Thomas. "*And,*" the little boy went on, louder this time, fixing the audience with a stern look, "he plans to take up residence in Murriundah where he will write words for other singers to sing..." Thomas paused, giving Nick a quick glance before grinning at Lauren, "...while spending the rest of the time with his family. If his family will have him?"

Lauren mouth fell open. She couldn't help it. Her mouth fell open and she gaped at Nick. Really gaped at him.

He grinned at her, and then turned and looked at her son, *his* son, standing to the side of the assembly area. "Josh, you haven't changed your mind about letting me marry your mum since last night, have you?"

Lauren's heart smashed into her throat.

Josh grinned back at Nick. "Depends. You haven't changed your mind about giving me guitar lessons, have you?"

Nick shook his head.

Lauren watched their son's grin turn to a smile so genuine in its joy it was all she could do not to sob. "In that case, go for it, Dad."

It was Nick's turn to smile. He returned his gaze to her face, reached into the back pocket of his jeans and pulled out a little red velvet box.

Oh God. Oh God, this is happening. This is really happening.

He held her stare and lifted the lid off the box, revealing a ring made from a bright green pipe cleaner topped with a pink, plastic stone she recognised from the bottom of her class's goldfish tank.

"Thought I'd let you pick your own," he said, and everyone laughed. Well, Lauren assumed everyone was laughing. To be honest, she wasn't paying them any attention. Not when Nick was making his way toward her. Not when he was weaving his way through the mass of cheering students all clapping and calling out, "Go Nick!" and, "Go Miss Robbins," and chanting, "Kiss, kiss, kiss!"

Not when he was standing right before her, pipe cleaner ring in his fingers, his gaze on her eyes, his breath fanning her cheeks.

"Marry me, Miss Robbins? Be my plus one forever?"

She stared up at him, mouth open, pulse pounding.

Oh God. Should she say yes? Should she?

Are you kidding?

No. She wasn't.

She took the ring from his fingers and slid it on to hers. They could make it work. They *would* make it work. Because without Nick the rhythm of her life wasn't just wrong. It was incomplete. She understood that now. He made her laugh, he made her smile. He made her heart, her soul, sing. Her Nick. Not the world's anymore. Just...hers.

"You drive me mental, Nick Blackthorne," she whispered.

"You drive me crazy, Lauren Robbins," he whispered back, a second before he lowered his lips to hers and kissed her.

Just as the chanting, clapping, cheering students told him to.

About the Author

Lexxie's not a deviant. She just has a deviant's imagination and a desire to entertain readers with her words. Add the two together and you get wickedly fun erotic romances with a twist of comedy, sci-fi or the paranormal.

When she's not submerged in the worlds she creates, Lexxie's life revolves around her family, a husband who thinks she's insane, a cat determined to rule the house, two yabbies hell-bent on destroying their tank, and her daughters, who both utterly captured her heart and changed her life forever.

Contact Lexxie at lexxie@lexxiecouper.com, follow her on Twitter (@lexxie_couper) or visit her at www.lexxiecouper.com where she occasionally makes a fool of herself on her blog.

Let the games begin...

Suck and Blow
© *2011 Lexxie Couper*

Talent agent Frankie Winchester is a hellion. Her motto is all a girl needs is a fun time, a fast car and an awesome masseur on speed dial. There's only one person who could beat her at anything. Alec. Bane of her high-school existence, a kid whose parents were as working class and loving as hers were rich and distant.

When celebrity landscape architect Alec Harris spots Frankie at an exclusive Sydney house party, everything comes rushing back. The memory of being the "cheap-money" kid, trying and failing to prove himself—and impress his dream girl, Frankie Winchester.

Unexpectedly partnered in a wildly sexy game, the delicious friction ignites a scorching sexual tension. But there's more than a playing card trapped between them. Frankie refuses to admit that kiss shook her to the core. Alec wants nothing less than her full surrender.

Warning: C'mon, the book's called Suck and Blow. What more warning do you need?

Available now in ebook from Samhain Publishing.

Enjoy the following excerpt from Suck and Blow...

Someone ran into him. Hard. A firm, warm body slamming into his side as if the person hadn't been watching where they were going but was in a damn hurry to get where ever it was.

He stumbled to his left, a chuckle rising to his lips as he turned to face the someone, his hands instinctively reaching out to steady them on their feet, his fingers curling around biceps both smooth and firm.

And looked straight down into the wide, blue-grey eyes of Francesca The Gun Winchester.

Oh, boy.

His mouth went dry. Just like that. His mouth went dry and his breath caught in his throat. The precise moment their eyes met, ten years were wiped from his life and he was the flustered, horny teenager aching to impress the girl every guy at his school and hers wanted to date.

"Errrr..." He licked his lips, his pulse quickening as he watched her gaze track the path of his tongue.

Say something, you idiot.

"I'm not really sure," he murmured, his voice deeper and huskier than normal, "but I think you kiss better than I do."

The words fell from his lips, uninhibited by his befuddled schoolboy's brain, each one making his heart beat faster. Jesus Christ, Harris, you are an idiot.

He couldn't stop looking at her. He couldn't remove his hands from her arms. He couldn't let her go. She was right here before him, staring at him with an expression he didn't have a hope in hell of deciphering on her exquisite face. Her smooth skin was warm against his calloused palms, her soft, sweet perfume threading into his body with every breath he took.

Christ, Harris. Do something, will you?

But before he could, Frankie raised one straight eyebrow and lifted her chin. "I don't think we can be certain based on one kiss, do you?"

Alec's heart slammed hard into his throat. "In that case," he said, lowering his head a fraction closer to her, "you better kiss me again."

"Should I now? Maybe you should be the one to kiss me?"

"And have you say I beat you once again?" He shook his head, enjoying their banter far too much. His balls ached and his dick was so hard it hurt. He wanted to kiss her like hell, but here he was—as usual—loving the sound of her voice.

Storm-grey eyes studied him from behind half-lowered lids, a small grin playing with her lips. "Should I go find a playing card again? Will that help?"

"Depends? Do you need a Ten of Hearts to hide behind?"

One dark, straight eyebrow lifted. "I don't hide from anything."

"And yet, I'm noticing a distinct lack of kissing going on here."

"Maybe you're not as clever with that tongue of yours as you thought?"

He chuckled. "To quote someone very close to me, 'I don't think we can be certain based on one kiss, do you?'."

Frankie's chin tilted. "In that case, you better kiss me again."

Alec lowered his head closer still to her upturned face. "If you insist, Fran—"

She didn't let him finish. Her lips found his and there was nothing chaste or hesitant about her kiss. She dipped her tongue into his mouth, swirling it around his. Her hands slid up his chest, her fingers resting lightly on his collarbone before, with a low groan, she pressed her body to his. Her breasts crushed against his chest, sending dizzying waves of pleasure through him. Her thighs moved against his legs, their smooth, leather-encased length playing with his senses. Ten years ago those legs had been the stuff of his unbidden fantasies—legs both soft and toned he'd imagined wrapped around his waist. Now, it wasn't just his waist he wanted them wrapped around. Now, he wanted them wrapped around his head as his tongue explored the sweet, damp slit of her pussy.

Now, he wanted...

She rose up onto her tiptoes, stroking the stiffening pole of his cock with the soft mound of her groin, sucking his tongue into her mouth as she did so and it was his turn to groan.

Jesus, she was driving him wild.

His hands raked her back. He wanted to touch her. All of her.

It takes more than a rock star to rock your world.
Sometimes you need a friend.

Tropical Sin
© *2011 Lexxie Couper*
A *Bandicoot Cove* Story

McKenzie Wood has just spied her ticket out of tabloid journalism. A rumor-shrouded rock star who thinks he's incognito at Bandicoot Cove resort. With a little help from her BFF she'll be on her way to serious work in no time. Aiden's perfect for the job—pulse-pounding gorgeous, and probably gay. After all, she's never seen him date anyone.

Aiden Rogers admits it's pretty damned pathetic that he can rush into burning buildings, but not have the guts to tell McKenzie he's in love with her. No way can he tell his best friend he'd like to do some seriously sinful things to her, especially since she's never shown one iota of sexual interest.

Nick Blackthorne looks forward to some "unfamous" downtime in his home country. He's surprised to find his creative muse stirred—more like brought to rigid attention—by a couple so sexy that all he can think about is the three of them. Together.

Three bodies move together as one, and the music becomes a smoldering beat that rivals the island's heat. When the truth inevitably comes out, the heat might be enough to save three souls...or end up just another sinner's lament.

Warning: One plus one plus one equals OMG sex, are-you-freaking-kidding-me orgasms and some serious mind-blowing climaxes.

Available now in ebook from Samhain Publishing.

Enjoy the following excerpt from Tropical Sin...

Aidan didn't just scramble from the bed; he leapt from it. He stared hard at the rock star leaning in the threshold, his heart thumping fast. "What the fuck are—?" he began, a second before Nick's gaze slid to him and he realized he was standing in the middle of a hotel room with his tackle—still semi-hard and probably glistening with McKenzie's juices—on show.

Jaw clamping shut, glare locked on Nick's smiling face, he shoved his dick back into his cargos and yanked up his fly. What the hell was Nick Blackthorne doing here? And what the *hell* did he mean "join in"?

"Nick?" McKenzie's startled voice shattered the suffocating silence, and from the corner of Aidan's eye he saw her step back from the open door, her eyebrows dipping in a stunned frown. "I...we...you..."

She stammered over the personal pronouns, each one passing her lips in a short, breathless hiccup, her normal poise nowhere to be seen.

The rock star raised his eyebrows, a grin Aidan would have sworn was cheeky playing with his lips, if not for the hesitation in his eyes. And the uncertainty.

Nick himself, it seemed, didn't really know why he was here. Or what was going to happen next.

"How can we help you, Nick?" Aidan held the man's stare, a heavy beat thumping in his temple, his throat. If what the singer was going to suggest was what Aidan suspected...

An unbidden image flickered through his head, McKenzie, naked, pressed between them both, her head thrown back as both Nick's mouth and his own explored the perfection of her throat, her breasts.

His pulse quickened and his balls—so recently depleted—grew hard. Jesus Christ, what was he thinking?

"I came to ask..." Nick paused, rubbing at his mouth with a hand before raking it through his hair; hair, Aidan couldn't help but notice, much more messy than it had been at the bar. "I wanted..." He let out a harsh breath, shaking his head and stepping backward. "Fuck," he muttered, turning his face away, "where's the cool fucking rock star when I need him?"

Aidan's pulse beat faster. He narrowed his eyes, knowing he should do something, say something. But what? What exactly did he want to say?

Before he could work that out, however, Nick swung his stare back to them both, looking first at McKenzie and then Aidan, a calm resolution falling over his face. A face hundreds of thousands of women—and likely a few men—fantasized about over and over again. A face, when combined with a voice unlike any the world had heard, that elevated Nick Blackthorne beyond fantasies.

"I want to have a threesome," he said, that ambiguous accent almost all Australian now. "So fucking much I'm aching all over."

McKenzie's mouth fell open, but not before Aidan was at her side, his stare locked on Nick. "I think—" he started, but Nick cut him off, his gaze holding Aidan's with just as much force.

"I haven't heard music, lyrics, for a long time. Too long to remember." He let out a ragged sigh. "I haven't felt alive for a long time either. I've been dead inside for so long I'd forgotten what it was like to feel *anything*. But the second I heard McKenzie laugh—" he closed his eyes for a moment, an expression of sheer rapture crossing his face, "—the second I saw her in your arms..."

He opened his eyes and looked at Aidan, and that haunted, hesitant torment was back on his face. "I want to be a part of your intimacy."

Something heavy and hot surged through Aidan's veins, though his body. "What you're saying," he said, keeping his voice calm, modulated, "is you want to make love to the one woman you know I've wanted forever?"

McKenzie gasped. Nick's nostrils flared. "Yes," he nodded. "While you do as well."

"You want to…" McKenzie's unfinished question, uttered on a shaking breath, should have torn Aidan's stare from Nick's. But it didn't.

"I want to lose myself in the magic of your desire for each other," Nick continued, the words low and smooth, and yet at the same time rough and husky. "Just standing here now, looking at you both, looking at the room behind you…the rumpled sheets, the rumpled hair…the scent of your pleasure streaming into my body with each breath I take…" He closed his eyes again for a split second, shaking his head as if moved by something Aidan couldn't experience.

Or maybe already had?

"Arousing," Nick growled, and it was a growl. Guttural and barely controlled, it was the horniest sound Aidan had ever heard a man make. "So damn arousing."

He looked at them again. "I'm assailed by images of you both together. Ever since you left me at the bar, Aidan, ever since I knew you were coming back here to claim the woman of your dreams, I can't stop seeing you together, moving together… Fuck me, I can't stop wanting to be a part of that."

Aidan's mouth went dry.

"I don't want to intrude on your intimacy." Nick shook his head again, even as he moved his stare to McKenzie, his eyes beseeching. "I know you need time alone, but damn it, just for once, I want to be a part of something so very few people in the world ever get the chance to experience: true bliss."

He returned his stare to Aidan. "McKenzie is so fucking gorgeous." The sides of his lips twitched a little in a small smile. "And God help me, the thought of you making love to her..."

He left the rest of the sentence dangling between them, saying instead, "I hear music again. I feel it in my soul, but the song isn't finished." He paused again, his Adam's apple rolling up and down in his throat. "Just one day, that's all I ask. Just one day, the rest of *this* day. Please."

SAMHAIN PUBLISHING

It's all about the story...

Romance

HORROR

Retro ROMANCE

www.samhainpublishing.com

CPSIA information can be obtained at www.ICGtesting.com
Printed in the USA
BVOW012240200213

313841BV00002B/83/P